WHO WE COULD BE

CHELSEA M. CAMERON

GW00480734

Get Free Books!

Tropetastic romance with a twist, Happily Ever Afters guaranteed! You can expect humor and heart in every Chelsea M. Cameron romance.

Get a free book today! Join Chelsea's Newsletter and get a copy of Marriage of Unconvenience, about two best friends who get fake married to share an inheritance and end up with a lot of *real* feelings.

And now, back to Who We Could Be...

About Who We Could Be

Tessa O'Connell has everything she could possibly want. She's engaged, she has her dream job working at a bookstore, and she's going to be the maid of honor in her best friend's wedding next month.

Montgomery "Monty" Ford has everything she could possibly want. She's getting married in June, she worked hard to achieve her dream job as a librarian, and she's helping her best friend plan her wedding for next year.

Unfortunately, plans go seriously awry when Monty's fiancé ends up being a cheating loser and Tessa's engagement falls apart. The plans they made so carefully are in complete shambles, and they're both at a loss for how to move forward.

Tessa and Monty turn to one another to try and pick up the pieces, and what starts as an attempt to use each other for dating practice turns into something they never saw coming that will change everything they know about themselves and each other.

What happens when it turns out the one you really want has been standing in front of you the whole time?

For anyone who needs a Happily Ever After, this one's for you...

Chapter One

"I can't believe you're getting married in a month," I said as I licked ice cream off my arm. Monty had wrapped my cone in a napkin, but that hadn't stopped it from dripping on me. "Shit." Now it was on my shorts. The white ice cream looked like cum.

"Oh my god, you're hopeless," Monty said, pulling a wet wipe out of her purse and attacking my face.

"Stop it, I can do it myself," I said, trying to slap her hand away, but only succeeding in flinging the rest of my ice cream onto the grass. "Seriously?!" I was having bad luck with ice cream today.

"I'll get you another one," she said, but didn't cease wiping me down. I glared at her the whole time, but I knew fighting would only make it worse. Plus, I didn't want to walk around with a sticky face.

"There," she said, sitting back and contemplating her own ice cream, which was in a bowl with the cone stuck on top. Less messy.

Monty didn't like mess, which was bizarre considering that

1

she'd been my best friend since we were five, and I have always been a walking disaster.

I made a growling sound at her to show my displeasure at being cleaned off like a small child, but she just laughed and used my shoulder to push herself off the picnic table and went to order another cone for me. I scrubbed the ice cream off my shorts with a napkin, and then pulled Monty's ice cream closer and grabbed a spoon.

Monty came back and handed me the cone, but I wouldn't look at her face.

"Really?" she said as I swallowed the last mouthful.

"It was melting. I had to save it," I said, pointing at the empty bowl.

"Fine, then I'm eating this one." She grabbed the bowl and threw my replacement cone in it, holding it away from me.

"No, that's not fair!" I reached, but she was wily and slid away as families and groups of people at the other picnic tables stared at our shenanigans.

Monty held her hand out to stop me. "Cin, I literally bought this. It's mine." She knew she had me when she used that nickname. It had originated from the word "cinnamon," a nod to the color of my hair and the fact that I had gotten the spice confused with the word synonym in first grade and she never wanted me to forget it.

"Fine," I said, crossing my arms and sitting down.

"Are you going to pout for the rest of the day?" She sat down next to me. A few strands of her dark hair had escaped the messy braid that lay on her shoulder.

"Maybe. I'm thinking about it," I said.

Monty sighed and held the spoon out to me. "You can have a few bites."

I looked at the spoon.

"Do I need to qualify what amount counts as a bite, or can you just be an adult for five seconds?" she asked, eyes narrowing from underneath an enormous hat. I was the one who should probably be wearing a hat like that, with my paler skin and freckles, but it looked better on her anyway. I wasn't a hat person.

"No, I can be an adult." I took three reasonable bites and handed the bowl back to her.

"Thank you."

The diamond on her left hand caught my eye as she finished off the rest of the ice cream and nibbled on the cone.

"Are you ready? To be married and shit?" I asked. She hadn't answered me earlier.

"I'm as ready as I can be, I suppose. How much can you really prepare?" she said, before getting up and throwing our trash away. That was probably all she was going to say on that subject.

I looked down at my own left hand, where a ring should be. Where a ring *would* be if I wouldn't fuck up and lose Gus's grandmother's diamond ring that he'd slid onto my finger on New Year's Eve of this year.

I'd asked him if it was okay if I didn't wear it because I was so afraid of something happening to it. Right now it was safe and snug in my mother's jewelry box. Gus said he didn't care if I wore it, so that was good enough for me. Maybe he could get me a cheap band when we eventually got married. Whenever that would be. I had to get through Monty's wedding in one piece first.

"You ready?" she asked, interrupting my thoughts.

"Yeah." I looked up from my ringless hand.

Monty and I walked back across the street from the ice cream stand and up the road a little way to her apartment above the coffee shop. I was still broke as hell from three years of college and no degree, so I was crashing with my parents until I got married and moved in with Gus. I'd decided a long time ago that I didn't want to live with him until we got married and I was sticking to that.

Monty's place was tiny, but it was cozy, and I spent more time here than I did at my parent's house most weeks. Even with my older three brothers moved out, it was still a lot being twenty-four and having to tell your mom when you were going to be home.

I flopped on Monty's couch, which we'd found at a yard sale three years ago and was covered in dark green velvet.

"Are you still sure you don't want to do the whole bachelorette thing?" I asked as she hung up her hat and curled her feet up in the giant armchair that my aunt and her wife had given her from their antique shop.

"Yes, I don't know how much more clear I can be. I don't want to do that shit, Tessa."

I put my hands up in surrender.

"Okay, okay, I get it. I just didn't want you to regret anything later. I'm just doing my duty as MOH and BFF." There was no one else I would have allowed to be Monty's Maid of Honor, even if she'd had someone else in mind.

"It's fine. I'm just not into that," she said, tracing a fabric bird printed on the chair.

"I know, I know."

My phone buzzed with a text from Gus, just a funny meme. We had a date planned tonight, but all I wanted to do was sit on the couch and read or watch something.

Can we just chill at your place? I asked.

Yeah, no prob. See you at 8?

Yup, sounds good. I thought about it for a second and then added a heart emoji, but deleted it before I hit Send.

"You need to go?" she asked.

"Nope, just hanging out with Gus later, but I'm all yours for now."

4

Then her phone made a sound and I waited as she read the message and typed out a response, her forehead contracting.

"What's up?" I asked.

"Nothing, just TJ."

"Has he apologized?"

Monty sighed and shook her head.

"Not yet. I told him that I'm not compromising on this and he can do what he wants with that." Her fingers fluttered and she glanced down at her ring before snapping her eyes back up to meet mine.

"Are you sure you want to marry him?" It was a question I'd asked hundreds of times in hundreds of ways.

"Yes," she said, her voice sharp. "Yes, I am marrying him."

I wanted to argue with her, but we'd had this fight before and we never got anywhere.

"Please, can we not do this right now?" She pressed her fingers to her eyebrows, massaging, and I wondered if she was fighting a migraine.

"Yeah, okay," I said, getting up. "Do you need some ice?" Often if she put an ice pack on the back of her neck, it would help.

"No, I'm fine. Just stressing about getting everything done." Even throwing a small wedding was a monumental task, and it was almost here. She had a dress, we had a place, and in one month my best friend was going off into her new life.

I shoved those thoughts to the back of my mind and went to her cute kitchen to make her some tea.

A set of arms wound around me and a chin sat on my shoulder.

"Hey," she said.

"Hey," I said, pulling away to turn off the kettle.

"You okay?" she asked. I poured the water into two mugs and added the bags of tea and turned to face her.

"Are you sure, Ford?" I'd read about a character in a book

who called people by their last names when I was younger and thought it was cool, so I'd tried it out for Monty and it had just stuck. We'd been eight at the time.

She took the mug of tea from me.

"Yes, I'm sure. This is what I want." The linoleum of the kitchen floor was cool under my feet and the tea was hot in my hands.

"I don't believe you," I said, voicing the words that I'd been thinking since she'd told me she was marrying TJ and that she was happy with him.

"I don't need you to believe me, I just need you to be there for me, Tessa." She didn't look happy. She didn't sound happy. I knew her better than I knew myself and I *knew*. I also knew that I would never get her to change her mind. Montgomery Ford did not change her mind.

I gave up. "I'm always there for you, Ford. Always."

She put her hand on my shoulder and squeezed.

"Thanks, Cin."

"HOW MUCH DO you think Ford would hate me if I threw her a surprise bachelorette party?" I asked Gus as I lay on the couch with my legs in his lap. He passed the bowl of popcorn to me.

"I don't know, are you enjoying being alive?" I took my eyes from the screen and met his in the glow of the television. His brown hair flopped over his forehead, forever unruly.

"Yeah, yeah, I get your point." I tossed a piece in my mouth and crunched. "You didn't put enough butter on this."

"I could never put enough butter on it for you, Tess. If you had it your way, it would be butter with a side of popcorn." That earned him a handful of popcorn tossed in his face.

"Hey!" That earned me getting the bowl dumped on my

head, but I deserved it. A popcorn fight ensued and then he went for my hair.

"I will bite you," I said as he reached. Gus and I had known each other almost as long as Monty and I, and he knew how to push each and every one of my buttons.

He wiggled his fingers with menace and then started tossing the ruined popcorn back in the bowl.

"I really need to get a dog," he said.

"You should. Oh, can we have a dog, please?" I got down on my knees next to him and clasped my hands.

"Sure, we can get a dog. We can get as many dogs as you want." I helped Gus gather the rest of the popcorn from the floor and we ended up just sitting there with our shoulders touching, backs against the couch.

"You're so nice to me," I said with a sigh.

"You're not easy to be nice to. It's a fulltime job," he said, and I scowled, but he put his arm around me. I leaned into him and closed my eyes. Gus's familiar scent wrapped around me. A little bit of sweat, a little bit of the natural deodorant his mother made, a little bit of fabric softener. It was a safe smell, a cozy smell.

"Hey, you want to stay over?" he asked, and I opened my eyes.

"No, I should get home, it's late." That wasn't true, exactly, but I slipped out from under his arm and stood up. Gus rose to his feet and pulled me into a hug.

"Text me when you get there."

He was so tall, I spoke into his shirt. "Gus, I live seven miles away."

"Still." He let go and I headed to the door, waving as I left.

I thought about Gus as I drove home, taking the longer way that gave me some more time before I had to deal with my parents. We had always been an unconventional couple, Gus and I. We didn't have cute nicknames for each other, and both of us had made the promise not to live with someone or have sex before we were married. Not out of any sort of obligation, religious or otherwise, but it just seemed like a good idea. I'd made that decision in high school and he'd readily agreed. Sure, we kissed, but our relationship wasn't about all that stuff. We *got* each other, and I loved him. Plus, my family loved him. He'd been part of us since the beginning. It was only natural for him to join us in a more permanent way. I'd never thought of *not* marrying Gus.

I sat in my car for a minute to collect myself before I walked into my house. Donny's car was in the driveway, so I knew I was going to get attacked the minute I was through the door.

"Hey, you back from fooling around with your fiancé?" Donny's voice boomed through the living room and into the kitchen, where I'd come in the back door.

"Hi Donny," I said, cringing. I didn't need my brother talking to me about my (nonexistent) sex life. "How's Steph?" His wife of five years was due with their second child in a few months.

I walked into the living room to find Dad in his recliner and Donny and Mom on the couch. Dad blinked his eyes open, pretending that he hadn't already been sleeping. I flopped in between Donny and Mom.

Donny laughed. "I'm on pedicure duty now. I'm considering a second career in a nail salon. See?" He took his socks off and wiggled his toes that were painted with a sunset orange color.

"Pretty," I said, admiring them.

"Thank you."

"How's Gus?" Mom asked, looking up from the game on her phone.

"Good," I said.

"Is he good or is he *really good?*" Donny asked, wiggling his eyebrows. He and I had both inherited red hair from some recessive gene in our family tree.

"Donny, you're disgusting and you're lucky I don't poison you one of these days, but I'm scared of your wife."

Donny cackled. "That's fair, I'm terrified of her too." Steph had worked as a bouncer and now had one of those scary bootcamp workout gyms where she screamed at people to flip tires and shit. I went to her kickboxing class a few times a week. Mom and Donny talked about this and that and I let the soft sounds of home lull me until my eyes were heavy.

"I'm heading to bed," I said, getting up. Donny said he had to get home; he'd just come by to mess with the kitchen sink. I hugged him and both my parents before going to my room.

I'd forgotten to tell Gus that I'd arrived home safely, and I had a few missed messages from him, so I apologized and said I was going to bed.

After slipping on some undies and an old camp t-shirt, I crawled into bed with my phone. Moments before, I'd been ready to completely pass out, but now my brain was alert and needed something to do or else I was going to lay there and stare at the damn ceiling for a few hours until finally shutting down.

I did a little bit of checking and reading and scrolling. I knew exactly what I wanted, and that was to talk to Monty, but it was too late for that. TJ was probably there, or she was already asleep and I didn't want to bother her. Just as I was about to start looking up my former high school enemies on social media, a text from Monty came in.

You awake?

Chapter Two

MONTY

TJ had come and gone. He claimed he had to get up early, which was true, but also, he could have stayed. I hoped when we moved in together just before the wedding that things would settle into a new pattern. I'd been mentally preparing myself for the changes, but I didn't know how much you could really prepare for every single facet of your life changing.

I'd be moving to a new place that I'd have to share with another person. Sure, I'd lived with my parents, but it had been just us. Sharing a home with a husband was different than sharing a home with your parents. I didn't need to move in with him to know that.

I made some tea and wandered around my apartment, reaching out and touching my things. A lot of this stuff would have to go, and not because TJ wanted me to get rid of everything, but we would have to buy things together. Instead of things being mine, they would be *ours*.

My mother had already started buying us things, and I had a little pile going in one corner. A crockpot, a dish set, some towels. None of them were to my taste, but they were free, so I wasn't going to turn them down. She'd even started making me a quilt for our bed, but I wasn't holding my breath to see the thing finished. Mom didn't have a whole lot of follow-through.

Unable to sleep, I lay on the couch and pulled a blanket over myself. I could read or watch something, but I didn't think my mind could hold onto anything long enough to focus. There were so many thoughts and worries and questions about the wedding, my marriage, what kind of a wife I was going to be.

I wanted to talk to Tessa, to tell her everything. To open up all the doors and let her see my ugly thoughts as she stroked my hair and told me it was going to be okay.

I was still upset about our fight earlier. She was trying and I loved her for caring, but no one was ever going to be good enough for me, in her opinion. TJ was a good guy. My parents adored him, and he was everything they'd ever want in a son-in-law. He'd asked my dad's permission before proposing, which I guess I was supposed to think was romantic, but I just thought was annoying and patriarchal.

Whatever, that didn't matter. I was marrying him because that was the plan. It was my plan, it was his plan, and it was my parent's plan. I loved him, I did.

Tears itched at the corners of my eyes. I needed to think about something else. I pulled out my phone and texted Tessa. Something told me she would be up.

You awake?

She responded immediately and I felt myself smiling.

Everything okay?

Yeah, I said. **Just can't sleep.**

I flinched as she sent me a request for a video chat. I answered as fast as I could, my fingers slipping on the screen and almost dropping my phone.

"Hey," I said. She was in her room and it was dark, her face lit by the flickering of the TV that was on mute.

"Hey," her voice was soft. "You want to talk about anything? Or talk about nothing?" If there was one thing Tessa O'Connor was good at, it was talking.

"Nothing, please."

That made her grin.

"Got it. Did you know that the inventor of Cornflakes made them to stop people from masturbating?"

I blinked at her for a few seconds.

"I did not," I replied.

"He was religious and thought that getting yourself off led to all kinds of bad things, and that certain foods would inspire you, or whatever, so he made Cornflakes and threw a hissy fit about not adding any sugar because sugar makes you horny, or something."

"He sounds like he was fun at parties," I said, trying to imagine him pitching the idea.

"Oh, definitely. Apparently, he never had sex with his wife either," she said.

"I'm not sure if I should feel good or bad for her." That made her laugh.

"Same. Need something else?"

I burrowed further into the couch.

"Yes, please."

I listened as Tessa told me about other breakfast cereal origins. I had no idea how she remembered all of that, but Tessa's brain was an entire library's worth of information. I never knew what she was going to pull out, and I was never bored with her. It was impossible to be bored around Tessa.

"You know, there are podcasts for this," she said, and I snapped my eyes open. I'd started to drift off.

"True, but none of them are narrated by you," I said.

She yawned.

"That's true. I do have a good voice." She did. Tessa yawned again. It was time to let her sleep. We both had to work tomorrow, her at a used bookstore, me at the library next door. Incredible that we'd somehow end up working right next to each other all these years later when we were paired up as Line Buddies in the first grade.

"Goodnight, Ford," she said in a drowsy voice. She'd been calling me that forever, and I'd given up on trying to get her to stop. I was just used to it now. Sometimes I even liked it.

"Goodnight, Cin," I said. It was only fair that I gave her a nickname that annoyed her right back.

Figuring that sleeping on the couch was probably bad for my back, I rolled to my feet and fumbled my way to my bedroom. For the millionth time, I wished I had a cat or some sort of animal, but TJ was allergic, so pets weren't an option for me. Having someone to cuddle would have made me feel a little less alone.

Part of me considered calling Tessa back, but that would be ridiculous. I could get through a night without her. I'd gotten through many nights without her.

Soon I wouldn't be alone. Soon I would be with TJ, for the rest of our lives. Just the two of us.

I NEEDED SO much coffee the next day to make it through. I was just thinking I needed another cup to take me through the afternoon as I reshelved some books and kept my eye on some teens on the computers at the same time.

"Hey Ford," a voice said behind me, too loudly.

Instantly I turned around and shushed a smirking Tessa, who crossed her arms and leaned on the bookshelves.

"You've really got your shush down, I'm so proud." Her hair was all over the place from being outside on this windy day. Her undercut was growing out again, which meant she was probably here to pout and beg me to shave it for her. She thought she was being sneaky, but Tessa was about as sneaky as a punch to the face.

"What can I do for you?" I said, putting on my best librarian voice.

"I was just coming over to see if you needed any coffee. I was running over to get some and thought I'd be a good best friend and ask."

I slumped against the shelf.

"Yes, I definitely need coffee. So bad."

Tessa pointed at me with finger guns. "You got it. Be right back."

I finished shelving the books, checked on the teens, and went to the break room in the back and propped the door open so Tessa could come in. Technically speaking, coffee wasn't allowed in the library, so we always consumed it in the break room.

Lindsey, the head librarian, was on her computer in her attached office and looked up to give me a smile. I was really lucky to get to work for her, and she always stepped up when a patron was being a problem and wanted to Speak to a Manager. She also didn't put up with nonsense from anyone. She'd come in like a tornado, whipping this small-town library into shape.

"Knock knock," Tessa said, before poking her head through the door and presenting me with a sweating, plastic cup and a bag with what I supposed were pastries in it.

"My hero!" I said, pretending to swoon.

"You can't swoon until I've put my stuff down so I can catch you," she said, setting everything on the counter. There was a rapping sound and we both turned to find Lindsey watching us through the glass window in her office.

"No swooning," she said.

"Yes, ma'am," I said, saluting her before picking up my coffee and sucking some through the straw. "Ahhh, sweet elixir of life. How many shots are in this?" I checked the side but there were only two. I narrowed my eyes at Tessa.

"Hey, don't growl at me, you know that you can't have that much caffeine in the afternoon because then you're up all night and who are you calling to talk to sleep? Me." She pointed to herself. "So this is for your own good, as well as mine."

I scowled and sipped my drink.

"You're sassy today, what's up?" Tessa hopped up on the counter and dug through the paper bag, unearthing a cherry Danish that she proceeded to devour.

"Not enough caffeine," I said, holding up the drink.

Pastry finished, she licked her fingers and looked at me, frosting and cherry goo glistening on her lips. I reached behind me for a napkin from the container on the table in the middle of the room, handing it to her.

She wiped her face and tossed the napkin in the trash on the other side of the room.

"Anything else bothering you?" she asked, leaning forward. I took a step back and leaned against a chair.

"Not really. Just everything." I waved one hand vaguely.

"Okay," she said, hopping off the counter. "Well, I should probably get back to work, that took me more than fifteen minutes. Come over after you get off if you want."

"TJ's coming over," I said, and Tessa made a face for a split second before hiding it. I knew she didn't like him, but she was going to have to get over it. I'd picked him and she was my best friend. I was not choosing between the two of them, now or ever.

"Sounds good," she said in her false cheery voice. "Bye." She was gone before I could thank her for the coffee.

15

WORK FINALLY ENDED and I went home to freshen up before TJ picked me up in his truck.

"Hey," I said, climbing up. He smelled like cigarettes, even though he swore he'd quit.

"Hey," he said, giving me a quick kiss and then gunning it up the street. There wasn't a whole lot to do around town, so we had to drive a little bit of a distance to get to TJ's favorite sport's bar. It wasn't my choice of date venue, but he was always happier there, so I didn't mind compromising.

The crappy radio blared country music as I tried to talk to him. He was in one of his moods, so I gave up after a little while. I kept stealing looks at him. There was one thing about TJ: he was handsome as hell. Clear blue eyes, cheeks that were always just a little bit ruddy, and a dimple in his chin. By all objective standards, he was hot.

We made it to the bar at last and went in. He'd made a reservation this time, so that was nice. Last time we'd had to wait forever.

"Hey, so you should probably start moving some of your stuff over this weekend," he said, as I stared at a menu that I'd memorized for how many times I'd been here.

"Okay. I'll pack a few boxes up this week and have them ready. I also have those books for your mom." TJ and his parents had a rocky relationship, but they'd gotten closer lately, and I did like his mother. I'd picked up a few used books I thought she might like. Seemed like the thing to do for my future mother in law.

"Yeah, sounds good."

TJ ordered a beer and messed on his phone as I tried to engage him in any conversation. Finally, I got him talking about movies. TJ loved movies. I'd never met anyone who had seen more movies than him. It was usually what we did on our dates. When we'd first gotten together, he'd take me out in his truck, set up a projector and a sheet on the side of a building and we'd watch them for hours and dissect them afterward. I couldn't remember the last time we'd done that.

"You want to go this weekend to see that new one? I can't remember the name."

"Can't. I've got to work, sorry. I'm pulling overtime for the wedding and everything," he said, not looking up from his phone.

Our wedding was nothing fancy, but that didn't mean it was free. Neither of us had a ton of funds, and I refused to let either of our parents put up any money to support us. We were both adults and we didn't need them to give us a cent. TJ was reluctantly on board with that plan, so he'd pick up some extra hours at his job, and I saw him a lot less.

After the wedding, things would calm down and we'd get back into our routine. We just had to get through the wedding. Only a few weeks left. I wish eloping wouldn't kill both sets of parents, or else I would have suggested that. It would have been so easy to just drive to the courthouse and be done with it. I could have worn my dress anyway, and Tessa could have stood by my side. Her condition on being my maid of honor was that she got to choose what she wore, and I still had no idea what her outfit was going to look like, no matter how many times I'd tried to get it out of her. When Tessa actually put in the effort, she could keep a secret better than anyone I knew.

TJ's gloomy mood forced me to not order dessert, even though they actually had decent cake at this place. He paid and we got back in his truck and I tried to bring him back around. I received one-word answers and grunts all the way back to my place.

He did get out and open my door for me and help me down from the truck.

"Thanks for dinner," I said. "You want to come up for a few minutes?"

He jammed his hands in his pockets and rocked back on his heels. His boots were covered in sawdust from work.

We hadn't had sex in weeks. I told myself it was because he was busy, but it was also me not making an effort. This man was going to be my husband and the least I could do was show him that I wanted him.

I leaned forward and grabbed his shirt so I could kiss him. He kissed me back, but pulled away quickly.

"Listen, I'm really tired. I'll make it up to you next week, I swear. Work is just a lot." I knew that, but it still stung when he kissed my cheek and got back into his truck and roared away.

Maybe next week.

Chapter Three

TESSA

"What about this?" Vanessa, my aunt said, pointing at a chair.

I shook my head. "No, that's not going to work. She doesn't need a chair." The two of us weaved through the antique shop, making our way to the back, where Vanessa's wife, Hollie, was dusting.

"Any luck?" she said, looking up from a shelf of plates.

"Not really." I sighed heavily and leaned against an antique bureau that had several items on it. "I just don't know what to get her. Nothing seems right. I've never had this much of an issue getting Ford a present before." I'd been hitting it out of the park until now.

For some reason, finding a wedding present for Monty was proving to be an impossible task. I'd thought that I could get "something old" and quirky for her, but I wasn't having much luck.

"How goes the dusting, my love?" Vanessa said, giving her wife a kiss.

"Never-ending," Hollie said with a laugh.

"Hey, you signed up for this," Vanessa said, holding up Hollie's hand where an antique emerald ring glinted in the light.

"Yes, darling," Hollie said, kissing Vanessa on the cheek. I loved seeing the two of them together. They'd only been married for a few years, but had been together as long as I could remember. I'd spent my childhood rampaging through the antique store with them chasing after me and pleading with me not to break anything. They never got mad when I inevitably did. Seeing them together was like seeing a matched set. They fit so perfectly, with Hollie tucked under Vanessa's arm.

"Look around," Vanessa said, her arm around Hollie, one hand playing with Hollie's brown curls. "See if anything strikes your fancy. Don't think about finding the right present, just think about something she'd like. A regular present, without the pressure of it having to be the perfect wedding present." That made sense.

I took my time going through the shop, trying to take everything in. The place was crowded, but organized and clean. The furniture all smelled of lemon polish and I always associated that smell with warmth and comfort. I walked past the corner with the books, where I used to hide and read when my aunts babysat me. My eyes meandered, looking at clocks and paintings and dishes and dolls. Monty would kill me if I bought her a creepy doll that was probably haunted, no matter how funny it would be to watch her open it.

No, joke gifts were not going to fly. I had to get her something special and personal. Everyone else was getting shit off her registry, but I didn't play that game. This woman was my best friend, and I was not getting a present that just anyone could get her.

Something caught my eye and I saw a tiny silver tea set. It

was only enough for two cups, but it was shiny and pretty and embossed with roses.

"Aunt V? I think I found something," I called and waited for my aunts to join me. I looked at the price tag and winced. Ouch. Good thing I'd set money aside for this.

"What you got there?" Vanessa said, peering over my shoulder. I pointed at the tea set.

"Oh, that's gorgeous, she's going to love it. You should get her some cloths and silver polish too. We got that off an estate sale," Hollie said, putting her chin on Vanessa's shoulder.

"It's yours," Vanessa said, hugging me. I leaned in and inhaled the scent of lemon polish and something just a tiny bit musty.

"No way, I'm paying for it," I said, as Hollie picked up the set and went to wrap it and put it in a box for me to take.

"No way, you're not paying for it," Vanessa said. "And that's final." Her hazel eyes narrowed, and she crossed her arms.

"But—" I tried to argue, but she put both hands on my shoulders.

"Listen, this is a present from you and from us. We love Monty, so consider it a joint present."

I couldn't really argue with that. "Fine. But I'm putting your names on the card."

"Deal," Vanessa said, as we walked toward the front and the door dinged with the arrival of a new customer in search of treasures.

Hollie put the box in my hands and I thanked both of them for the gift.

"We'll see you for dinner tomorrow night?" I balanced the box as I pushed through the door.

"Yup," I said. Every other Sunday I had dinner with my aunts. They said it was to rescue me from being raised with three older brothers, which I appreciated.

I took the present home and put it in my room before driving to Monty's place.

"Hey, it's me," I called as I walked through the door. I had a key, but it wasn't like she ever needed to lock her door. This was rural Maine. You were more likely to lose your key and have to call a locksmith than have someone break in. Fortunately, the local locksmith was really nice and if you invited him in for coffee and let him yammer a little bit about his life, he usually forgot to charge you. Not that I had any experience with that or anything.

"Do you ever knock?" Monty said, coming around the corner, oven mitts on.

"I thought about it, but then I didn't," I said. "Something smells amazing." Monty jumped and ran back into the kitchen and I followed.

"Yeah, I'm making a pie." Of course she was.

"What kind?" She pulled said pie out of the oven and it was a work of art. She'd done an elaborate braided lattice on the top. Carefully, she set the pie on a cooling rack near the small window. The curtains softly fluttered from the steam of the pie.

"Cherry," she said. "I'd say you can have a slice, but this is for Linda." TJ's mother. She wiped her forehead with her arm and set the oven mitts down. "But I had enough crust and filling left over to make a few mini pies. I just have to finish the crust."

I spied another tray of unfinished pies. "Can I help?" I went to the sink and washed my hands.

"Sure," Monty said, and we stood together over her tiny dining table where she had a wooden board laid out, covered in flour.

"Will you get mad if I fuck them up?" I asked, as she pushed a ball of dough toward me. Let's just say that I'd tried to bake and cook with her many times before and it hadn't gone that well.

"I'm not going to get mad," she said, but I gave her a look. "Okay, I'll try not to get mad."

"I'm going to hold you to that," I said as I started to roll out the dough. I sort of knew what I was doing, but I could feel Monty vibrating with anxiety next to me.

"Okay, I know you're not getting mad, but I can feel you stressing, Ford. What does it matter if the crust is perfect? I'll eat the ones that don't look good. It's the least I can do." The dough looked relatively flat, so I started cutting out strips.

"You're not going to measure?" Monty squeaked.

"No, I'm going for a rustic look," I said, and watched her eye start twitching. Sure, if I was making a pie for someone else, I might have been a little less haphazard, but winding Monty up was part of the fun.

I swiped a flour-covered finger under her eye.

"You're twitching, Ford." Monty slapped my hand away and pressed both hands onto the board and closed her eyes.

"Shut up," she said, and there was a tension in her voice that didn't seem to have anything to do with me messing up pie crust.

"Hey," I said, putting a floury hand on her shoulder. Monty wore an apron that looked like it was ripped from the corpse of an exhausted 1950s housewife. I already had flour all over my clothes somehow. "You okay?"

"Yeah, I'm fine," she said, flexing her fingers and rolling her shoulders back. "I'm fine."

"You know, the more you tell me you're fine, the less I believe you." Monty shrugged my hand off her shoulder and walked to the rack to stare at the finished pie.

"I'm fine," she said again. "Can you just not pester me right now, okay? I have a lot going on. I need to pack up some of my stuff and start moving it over to TJ's."

That last sentence made my stomach drop. I'd been ignoring the fact that she was going to be moving in with TJ after the wedding. I didn't want to think about the fact that I couldn't just show up at her place and crash on her couch or annoy her whenever I wanted like I did now. Things would be different, and I didn't like different. I didn't like it at all.

But I swallowed all of those feelings and asked, "Do you need any help?"

Monty shook her head.

"No, it's fine. I'm not going to take much. We're going to get new stuff, so most of my furniture is going to be donated."

I couldn't express how much I hated that she had to get rid of her stuff, but I guess it made sense. She'd buy shit with TJ and it would be romantic. Made me nauseated to think about that too. There wasn't much about her upcoming nuptials that didn't make me want to hurl my guts out. Ugh. I needed to talk about something else.

"Are you sure you can't let me have one slice? Just say your dog got it," I said, inching toward the pie.

"I don't have a dog," she said in a deadpan voice.

"You have no sense of imagination," I said.

Her eyes narrowed and I could see her fighting a smile. "You mean lying."

"Lying is just being creative with reality. And if you believe it enough, it's not a lie." I reached toward the pie with one finger and I heard a sound behind me.

"You put your finger in that pie, and you will be in trouble, Cin." Monty's voice was soft, but she held her rolling pin like she knew how to use it.

I moved my finger infinitesimally closer.

"What are you gonna do, Ford?" I didn't know why I loved teasing her this much, but it seriously gave me life. It was one of my favorite hobbies, next to kickboxing and reading really smutty fanfic.

Monty closed her eyes and inhaled slowly as I waited. Then her phone rang, startling us both.

"Freeze," she said, pointing the rolling pin at me. I did, and she answered her phone.

"Hey, yeah, what's up?" I knew who she was talking to just by the tone of her voice. I knew all of Monty's voices. She was talking to TJ. Instantly I stepped away from the pie and leaned against the counter.

Monty talked briefly to TJ and then ended the call.

"Sorry, he was just calling to figure out when I can bring stuff over tomorrow and then we're having dinner with his parents." Another roll of nausea. I didn't want pie now.

"How nice," I said, because I had to say something.

"You don't have to finish these. I can handle them." She went back to working on the mini pies and I went back over to join her.

"No, I can help. It's the least I can do."

"Thanks, Cin," she said, and I brushed another streak of flour on her cheek.

"You're welcome, Ford."

"CAN I HELP?" I asked, as Vanessa and Hollie flitted around the kitchen making dinner.

"No, no, we've got this," Vanessa said, waving a hand that had a spatula in it. Hollie pushed a glass of wine into my hand.

"Sweetheart, can you hand me that colander?" Hollie dashed to help Vanessa with a giant pot of pasta.

"You two really need to get some kids soon because there's no way I'm eating all that," I said.

"We're working on it," Vanessa said, brushing some dark hair out of her face. "Adopting while trans and gay can be a little tricky, but we think we might be getting closer." Hollie hugged Vanessa and kissed her on the cheek.

"Well, you're the best moms I know. Don't let my mom hear me say that." They both held their arms out to me and folded me in for a squeeze.

"Now, this carbonara isn't going to eat itself," Hollie said, her eyes a little misty. My stomach growled as if in response and we all laughed.

I'd set the table in the dining room with their good china and we said a quick grace before I started attempting to twirl pasta with my fork and a giant spoon and giving up. I didn't know how many times Vanessa had tried to teach me how to do this, but it just didn't work out.

"So, how's work going?" Hollie asked, eating as daintily as a queen. Or as daintily as I imagined a queen ate. I had no point of reference.

"Good. I'm somehow in charge of the Pride display, so if you have an ideas or suggestions, I'm all for it."

The bookstore kept giving me too much power and I didn't know how far I could push them before they realized that giving me any kind control was a bad idea. To be fair, the bookstore was owned by gay husbands, but they always did a subdued display.

This year was going to be their queerest Pride display. No half-assed, lukewarm rainbows this year. I'd been celebrating Pride as an ally since before I could remember. My aunts had taken me and my brothers to parades wearing "I love both my trans aunts!" t-shirts that my brother Mike had drawn the designs for. I still had them all in my closet. One of these days I'd make them into a quilt or something.

Vanessa and Hollie made suggestions and I ended up writing some of them down in my phone. I really wanted to do the window justice this year.

While I was working on my second piece of black forest cake, I got a call from Monty.

"Hey, I'm just at my aunts, what's up?"

The only thing I heard in response was crying.

"Oh my god, Ford, what's wrong?" I shared a terrified look with my aunts as all the possibilities chased each other through my brain. Car crash. Cancer. Fire. Kidnapping.

"Ford, you have to talk to me," I said, pleading, and starting to cry myself.

"TJ cheated on me," she finally got out through sobs.

"Holy shit. Holy shit, Ford." I stood up and started pacing the room. "Okay, okay, I'll be right there. Listen, I'm coming." I set the phone to speaker, and Monty's sobs filled the dining room.

"I have to go," I said and gave my aunts quick hugs and told them I'd call later with updates and assured them that no one had died.

"I'm coming, Ford, I'm coming," I said over and over as I raced to her place. She was still crying, and I was so scared and the drive took forever. Fortunately, I didn't see many cars on the road and there was a spot right in front of her apartment. I slammed the car in park and raced up the stairs. The door was unlocked and I found her on the floor of the living room, curled up into a ball.

"Ford, Ford," I said, touching her shoulder. She just cried and I wrapped myself around her. I needed to know what happened, but I needed to get her out of this part first. And then I'd get to decide exactly how much pain to inflict on TJ as I slowly murdered him.

"It's okay, I'm here, I'm here." This was peak best friend duty. I held the broken pieces of Monty together so she didn't fly apart in a thousand pieces.

"I'm here and it's going to be okay." It wasn't going to be okay, but that didn't matter. It was just the thing I had to say. I rubbed her back and told her to breathe and held her tight as her body shook with tremors.

At last she started to quiet. My arms ached from holding her so tight, but I wasn't letting go until she told me to. If it took the rest of our lives, I was going to hold her together if she needed me to.

"I'm okay," she said in a soft voice that broke my heart a little bit. She moved to sit up and I let her, loosening my hold, but not letting go completely.

"Hey," I said, when she raised her head. Her hair was all in her face, so I used one hand to push it out of her eyes. She had snot running out of her nose and her eyes were so puffed they were almost swollen shut.

"Listen, I'm going to get you a cloth for your face, but I'm coming right back." If I'd been wearing a shirt with longer sleeves, I might have just used that, but today had been a scorcher, so I only had a tank on with no excess material.

Monty nodded and I rushed to the bathroom to grab a washcloth to wet with cool water. I wrung it out and brought it back to her. Monty sat still, a tear here or there still escaping her eyes to run down her cheek as I wiped each one away and cleaned the rest of her face.

"What do you need?" I asked. I hoped she would tell me that she needed me to end TJ's life, because that would be my fucking pleasure.

"Just stay with me?" Another tear appeared and I wiped it away with my finger.

"No matter what, always," I said. Monty fell into me and I put my arms around her as she burrowed into my shoulder, as if she was trying to hide.

We sat on the floor so long that my right leg went numb, but I would not fucking move until she told me to.

"He's been fucking someone else," she said, her voice muffled. I slammed my lips shut so I didn't interrupt her or make any kind of comment. "I only found out because he left his phone on the table and I saw a text. A text that left nothing to the imagination. I knew I shouldn't have picked up his phone, but that's his fault for not having a better passcode. I just...I never thought he would do this to me. How could he do this to me? We're getting married."

Not anymore they weren't. I'd known TJ was fucking trash, but I was standing by her side as long as he didn't do anything like this. But now? No, he was as good as dead. She couldn't forgive him for this, I didn't care what kind of excuses he made. There was no excuse for this. None.

To think of him throwing her away made me want to throw up. He had her and all he had to do was not fuck it up, and he couldn't even do that. Death was too good for him. I'd never had thoughts this murderous before in my life. Incandescent rage, brighter and hotter than the sun, simmered and tingled in my veins. I wouldn't have been surprised to see flames to sprout from my fingers.

"We *were* getting married," she said, and raised her head from my shoulder and sniffed. I handed her the washcloth again.

I finally spoke. "Did you confront him?"

"Yeah. He denied it, but then I showed him his phone and he couldn't deny it. He said it was one mistake, but I don't know how you can call fucking another girl for months one mistake. That's where he's been instead of working late. He's been with her."

I couldn't hold it in anymore. "I'm going to fucking kill him."

"No, you're not." Monty grabbed my arm and dug in with her fingernails. "You're not going to kill him, because I need you to help me get through this and you can't do that if you're in prison for the rest of your life."

"Only if I get caught," I said.

29

That made her huff out a little laugh. "You'd get caught, you're not nearly as sneaky as you think you are."

"Okay, so help me get away with it."

She shook her head. "No, you're not going to kill him. And I'm not telling you her name because I don't want you going after her. When I asked him if she knew about me, he said she didn't."

"But you're going to tell her, right?"

Monty pulled her hair over her shoulder and started braiding random pieces.

"I think I have to. I'd want to know if it was me. I just need to figure out how to say it. She might not even believe me. If he could lie to her about being engaged, think about what else he might have told her?" That was a good point, but we had to at least make an effort to save someone else from destruction at the hands of this poor excuse for a human being.

"You can figure that out later. Right now what do you want to do?"

Monty looked around her apartment and sighed.

"I don't really know. My entire world just fell apart and I'm supposed to be getting married in a few weeks, so maybe we should order some pizza, I don't know."

I couldn't help the laugh that escaped from my mouth.

"Let's get some fucking pizza."

Our town was so small that there was no such thing as delivery pizza, but I called in the order to the pizza place that was attached to the hardware store, Charlie's. There was another restaurant that had pizza, but Charlie's was better, hands down. The recipe for the sauce had been handed down, and I had no idea what made it so magic, but I would have pounded shots of that sauce if I could.

The two of us could have walked to Charlie's to pick up the pizza, but I didn't think that Monty was in a state to leave the apartment, so I took my care and made the two-minute drive.

It took me forever to pick up, because I had to shoot the shit with Wendy, the cashier, Rose, the owner, and several customers who were eating at the counter.

I interrupted Hank, a local yokel who didn't seem to have a job, but always had money, and made my escape.

"I would ask what took you so long, but I know what happens when you walk into Charlie's," Monty said, when I walked in much later with the cooling pizza.

"Sorry. I'm just really bad about cutting and running. I don't know what it is, but people seem to want to tell me their life stories." Monty took the pizza from me and held my chin with one hand.

"You just have one of those faces." She let go and went to the kitchen to grab some plates for the pizza. If I was in charge, we would have eaten it from the box while sitting on the floor, with maybe some paper towels, but Monty had always been classier than I was.

She started setting up her little table, but then she pressed her hands to the surface. "Fuck it. Let's do it your way. But we're using plates."

So we ate on the floor, but we used plates and actual napkins, and had sweet tea from wine glasses. I managed not to spill too much on her rug.

"I should just lay down a drop cloth or something when you come over," she said as we both attempted to scrub out a sauce stain.

"This is your fault for buying a beige rug. Who owns a beige rug? Honestly." I did my best and Monty came after me with the special stain spray. She didn't seem to want to talk about everything that happened with TJ, but I couldn't help but flinch every time I saw her left hand because the ring was still there.

"I wonder how much I could get for it," she said, freezing mid-scrub and staring at her hand.

"You might have better luck trying to hock the diamond than the entire ring. Not a whole lot of market for used rings. Bad luck, you know." I gave up on the rug and went back to shoving pizza in my face.

"Yeah, that's true. I guess I'm going to find out. Fucking hell, Tessa, we spent so much money on non-refundable deposits." She covered her face with her hands and groaned.

"Hey, hey," I said, putting the pizza aside and reaching for her shoulder. "Don't think about that shit. You don't need to worry about it. We'll take care of it. We'll figure it out." That part was going to fucking suck. I knew that she'd spent a lot of money that she didn't really have on this, and she wasn't going to get a lot of that back. On the bright side, TJ had spent a lot that he wasn't going to get back, so there was a small consolation there. Plus, he was still paying off the ring debt. I hoped he defaulted on the loan and ruined his fucking credit.

"I'm just so tired, Tess." Monty rolled onto her side and curled up into a ball.

I wiped my hands and then started stroking her long hair. She closed her eyes and sighed. "That feels really nice. I haven't said it, but thank you for being here. I don't know what I'd do without you."

"The feeling is mutual, Ford. This is for all those times you've saved my sorry ass. The least I can do is be here for you through this." Her eyes fluttered open and she gave me an exhausted smile that wasn't quite all the way there. I was going to make it my mission in life to get her to smile again.

Oh, and destroy TJ. Completely and utterly destroy. He was going to wish he was dead when I was done with him.

MONTY FELL asleep on the floor as I stroked her hair so I did my best to try and scoop her up and carry her to bed, but it didn't really work, so I had to wake her up a little and help her walk to her bedroom. I got her under the covers and she mumbled something, but I didn't catch it.

Once I was sure that she was asleep again, I backed out of the room and cleaned up the mess from the pizza and filled her water bottle with water and ice and brought it back to her. I also made sure she had her phone nearby.

"We'll figure it out," I whispered, before leaving her again.

There was no way I was going home, so I made up the couch for myself like I had hundreds of times before. Monty always kept fresh sheets and extra pillows in the "Tessa closet" as she called it. I also had a bunch of clothes and other things in there. I sent my parents and my aunts a quick text about what was going on and that I was staying with Tessa for the night to make sure she was going to be okay.

Let us know if you need anything, including hiding the body Aunt V said. I told her that wasn't necessary, but good to know.

I also did a deep dive on TJ's social media, but didn't see anything incriminating because he didn't post all that often. He must have had secret accounts he'd been using. Fuck, I hated him so much. There might have been some sort of satisfaction that all my suspicions about him had been confirmed, but that feeling was destroyed by the anger I had for the way he'd treated my best friend.

To pass the time, I started making a list of all the things we'd need to do, and people we'd need to call to cancel the wedding. Every now and then I kept glancing over at the piles of presents in the corner of the room. Yeah, those had to go. I hauled myself off the couch and took several trips down to my car and shoved the presents in the trunk. Monty could decide what to do with that shit later. We could build a bonfire in my parent's backyard or sell that shit online if she wanted to.

That task completed, I didn't have much else to do but sit

on the couch and come up with all the worst ways to torture TJ.

A sound from the bedroom made me get up and stand outside the door to make sure I'd heard correctly.

I knocked softly. "Hey, Ford, you okay?"

Chapter Four

Monty

He'd done it. He'd really done that. I'd stared at the extremely graphic text for a long time before I realized what it said and what it meant. Then I had no choice but to see what else these two had been saying to each other, and then I wished I hadn't looked at all.

My stomach rolled and heaved and I rushed to the sink, nearly tripping over a box on my way.

I'd heaved a few times and then heard the toilet flush and TJ came back out. I couldn't remember much after that. I know I'd screamed a lot and he'd acted like I was the one who was in the wrong, and I was pretty sure I had threatened to kill him at least once and then I'd gotten in my car and drove home and called the only person I knew could help me: Tessa.

You would have thought that I'd cried myself out earlier, but here I was, awake in my room and crying again.

"Hey Ford, you okay?" Of course she'd heard me.

"No," I said, pulling a tissue out of the box beside my bed. If I didn't start drinking some water, I was going to get completely dehydrated and shrivel up like a raisin.

Tessa came in and sat on the bed.

"What do you need me to do?" she asked. That was Tessa, always asking me what I needed.

"Water," I croaked, and she handed me the water bottle that I hadn't seen on the nightstand. My hands trembled as I took a drink, slopping cold water all over myself.

"Hey, that's my line," Tessa said with a laugh. She mopped me up with tissues as best she could, and I took a few more sips without incident.

"Thanks," I said.

"Do you need anything else? Do you need me to talk about shit?"

Nothing could make me feel better right now, but hearing Tessa go on about nonsense for a while might help my mind stop spinning for a little bit so I could let my exhausted body shut down for a little while.

Over and over, I thought of all the things that TJ had ruined. Our wedding, for one. Cancelling that was going to be a massive project. Then I had to tell my parents, which was going to be a nightmare. They loved TJ more than I did.

Then there was unloving him. I couldn't unbreak my heart, and mending it was going to be a task in itself.

Not to mention dealing with everyone's input about my relationship. I wouldn't be able to go anywhere without someone giving me a comment or a sad look or whispering behind my back. It was a wonder that people weren't knocking down my door now, demanding for me to spill the tea. Those questions would come. It would all come, and I'd have to deal with that too.

One little wisp of a feeling that had started stretching and opening in my mind, and if I didn't know what to call it, I might have said it was something like relief. There would be time to turn that over and figure it out. Later.

"Please talk about shit," I said, and closed my eyes.

She launched into a recap of a terrible reality show, complete with voice impressions and I had to open my eyes and watch her because she got totally into it. Honestly, I'd rather listen to Tessa tell me about a show or movie than see the thing myself. Her retelling was usually better.

I found my face relaxing, my jaw unclenching, and my body heading toward something like sleep. Something warm brushed my forehead and I thought it might be a kiss, but I also might have imagined it.

THE NEXT THING I KNEW, my alarm was going off, but it stopped before I could reach for my phone.

"Sorry, sorry, I should have turned that off," a voice said, and I cracked my still-swollen eyes open. "Hey."

"Hey," I said, my voice cracking. I felt like I'd been hit by a truck, then hit by a train, then maybe run over by a bunch of other vehicles. I reached for the water and downed the entire bottle in a few gulps. Everything hurt, especially my head. I had a bitch of a migraine brewing right between my eyes.

"Shit, it's Monday," I said. I had to work, and so did Tessa. "I have to get ready." My plans were foiled when I tried to stand and it didn't go very well.

"Hey, I don't think that's a good idea. I can call out and I think you should too. You know that Lindsey will understand. You never take sick time, you've probably got a ton saved up." She was right, but I hated to use a day for something like this.

"Fuck," I said, clutching my head. Both of my eyes had started twitching and the soft light in the room was hurting my eyes.

"Come on, lay back down." Tessa pushed me back into

bed. "I'm going to get you some more water and make something for you to eat, okay? I also need to perfect my dramatic story to tell Ron and Bill." Ron and Bill were the couple who operated the used bookstore that was affiliated with the library. They were both totally lovely and they adored Tessa, so I didn't think she'd have any problems on that front.

"You don't have to take a day off for me," I said. "I'll be fine."

Tessa's jaw clenched and she shook her head. "Not a chance I'm leaving you today."

Normally I would have fought her, but I didn't have the energy.

"Fine, whatever." I closed my eyes and lay back on my pillows. Tessa came back a while later with a plate of eggs and bacon and water and tea. The last thing I wanted to do was eat, but she'd made up the plate and brought napkins and everything. It was so sweet that I couldn't turn it down.

"What are you eating?" I asked, and she revealed a second fork.

"Whatever you don't finish."

That ended up being most of the plate. I got a few bites in, but I did drink all my tea and have another glass of water. Tessa brought me some headache meds and in a little while, I tried getting up again and had more success.

"What do you need me to do?" Tessa asked when I came back from the bathroom.

"I need you to stop looking at me like I'm fragile and going to break. I'm going to be okay," I said. I mean, I wasn't, but she needed to hear the lie.

Tessa sat down on my bed and sighed. "I'm sorry I'm not better at this shit." I collapsed next to her and lay back.

"You're amazing, Cin. I don't know what I would do without you." She lay back and turned on her side. Her hair was all goofy in the back from how she'd slept on it. I reached out to smooth it for her.

"First, I'm going to take a shower. Then I want to go somewhere away from here and do something that will make me forget for a little while. Then I want to drink a lot of alcohol." Tessa laughed and I felt my face trying to assemble a smile. I was trying.

"I know exactly where we should go." Tessa jumped to her feet and went to my bathroom to turn the shower on. It took forever to warm up.

"Are you going to tell me where we're going?"

Tessa held out a hand to help me up. I took it and she hauled me to my feet and shoved me in the direction of the bathroom.

"Surprises are fun," she said as she closed me in the bathroom.

"For you," I muttered under my breath.

TJ SENT me a text message while Tessa and I were in the car going to wherever she was taking us.

"Is that him?" she asked, glancing over at me and then back at the road.

"Yeah. He said he wants to talk."

"Well, I want him to be forced to eat his own organs, but we can't get everything we want. Give me that." She held out her hand that wasn't holding onto the wheel.

"What if there's an emergency?" I said, clutching my phone. I wasn't going to send a message to him, but there were other people I needed to keep in touch with.

"I'll give it to you if there's something important. Hand it over." Deep down, I knew she was right, so I gave her the phone.

"You're not going to pretend to be me and text him back, are you?" I said, instantly suspicious. That was exactly the kind of thing Tessa would do.

"No, I'm not going to do that. I'm not going to do anything but keep him from getting to you for today."

I sighed and looked out the window.

"Pick a playlist," Tessa said, handing me her phone. I scrolled through and found one she'd made that was my favorite and put it on so it piped through the car speakers.

"Where are we going?" I asked, picking at one of my nails. My ring glinted on my hand and I thought I was going to throw up looking at it, so I made sure Tessa wasn't watching as I slipped it off my hand and into my pocket. Now I just had to be sure that I wasn't going to lose it. When I got back later, I'd have to do some research on what to do with it. Returning it to TJ was not an option. I'd chuck it in the ocean first.

"We're going where we're going. Stop trying to ruin it. You'll like it, I promise." I wasn't so sure about that. In fact, I highly doubted it, but at least this was a distraction, at least for a few seconds.

Tessa stopped to get coffee and ordered without me even having to ask. She handed it over and I sipped the caffeinated goodness. I was feeling stronger already.

"Eat that too." She chucked a bag of croissants at me and I forced myself to choke down a few bites. Coffee was one thing, but food still wasn't really sitting well with me.

The playlist rolled through the songs that we loved, and I watched Tessa as she dramatically sang along to every single one. Her brain was not only filled with random facts, but it was full of hundreds of song lyrics. I'd seen her memorize an entire song after listening to it two or three times. Tessa's brain fascinated me.

"Here we are," she finally said. I honestly had no idea

where we were, but I could read the sign that said *Maine Cat Sanctuary*.

"You know I can't have a cat at my apartment, we've talked about this so many times." It wasn't that I didn't want one, someday. I loved animals.

"We're not going to adopt one. We're going to go pet some kittens. Come on." She got out of the car and wrenched my door open, a huge grin on her face. I still couldn't smile, but I appreciated her effort.

"Come onnnnn," she whined, heading toward the door.

"Okay," I said.

"SEE? ISN'T THIS AWESOME?" Tessa said as she put as many kittens as she could into her lap at once. They all gravitated toward her, like she was the cat whisperer. I'd seen her do shit like this before with lots of animals. She definitely had some kind of supernatural powers where that was concerned.

I had only been able to lure two kittens toward me. One was all-black with one tiny white sock, and the other had impressive ear tufts and multi-colored fur. The black one was asleep in my lap, and the other one kept lightly biting my hand if I stopped petting the top of its head.

All of the kittens were up for adoption, but that definitely wasn't a decision I was making today. Not in this emotional state.

"Yes, you're very cute," I said, picking up the bitey kitten. It meowed in my face and then tried to bite my nose. "You are a little troublemaker."

"Oh my goodness yes, what is wrong?" One orange furball had been screaming at Tessa and she picked up the sweet thing and put it to her ear.

"Oh no, and then what happened?" She pretended to listen as the kitten meowed over and over again. "That's terrible, I'm so sorry." She kissed the soft head and cradled the fluff to her chest.

"We redheads understand each other," she said. The kitten had stopped complaining and its eyes kept closing as if it was going to fall asleep.

"What am I going to do, Cin?" I whispered. Cute animals could only distract me so much.

"I'm going to help you cancel all that shit, and you're going to send a message to that girl, and then you're going to move on. Because he's not worth it. He's not worth it. He never has been." Her tone was bitter, and I could tell it wasn't just from the cheating.

"I know you've never liked him," I said. "You aren't as subtle as you think you are."

"How was I supposed to like him?" Her voice startled all the kittens and they cried. "I'm sorry." She apologized and gave them all kisses. "But it's true. He wasn't even worthy to fix your car, god Ford. How did you expect me to feel?" She lowered her voice, but her tone cut me like knives.

"I expected you to support the decision I made."

Tessa rolled her eyes. "Clearly, he was a bad fucking decision."

I sat up, startled. "Are you blaming me for him cheating?"

"No, of course not! I'm just saying he wasn't a good guy, even without that. He's not good enough for you." Now I was the one rolling my eyes.

"So, who is good enough for me, because that's what you've said about anyone I tried to date." I rolled through the guys I'd told her I was interested in that she had shot down. The list was pretty long. True, a lot of those guys were losers, but still. She should let me make my own decisions.

"That's because no one is good enough for you, least of any of the crusty local guys."

"Tessa, that's ridiculous and you know it." She gently dislodged the kittens in her lap and stood up.

"The fact that you can't see yourself makes me so angry. You're amazing and you can't even see it. You sell yourself short all the time and I'm so tired of it. You deserve better. You deserve the best. I don't know who that is but admit one thing: you were never happy with TJ. Just admit that, because we both know it's true." Those words slashed me open, laid me bare. I couldn't do this anymore.

I put the kittens down and stood up. "I'll be in the car."

Why was she doing this? She was supposed to be helping me feel better, not making me feel more like shit. I got in the car and slammed the door shut. I'd thought I was out of tears, but there they were again. It took a few minutes before Tessa walked out and got in the car with me.

"I'm sorry. I shouldn't have said that."

I wiped my cheeks. "No shit you shouldn't have said that."

"I'm sorry," she said again, and I looked over and saw that she was crying too. "I just hate him for doing this to you."

"Yeah, well, that makes two of us."

We sat in the car, both silently crying for a while. Tessa swiped at her face, turned on the car and pulled out.

"Where are we going?"

"To get some alcohol," she said.

BOTH OF US decided that going to a bar wasn't the best idea, mostly because then we'd have no way to get home, so we headed instead to the closest gas station that sold booze. Tessa went in and grabbed whatever, coming out with two bags.

"Getting wasted isn't cheap, holy shit. But at least it's cheaper at home than at a bar."

Since neither of us wanted to get drunk at her parent's house, we headed back to my place. I kept getting distracted by a rattling in the trunk that had just been getting progressively worse the longer Tessa drove.

"What is going on back there?" Her car was ancient and prone to odd noises, but this was something else.

"It's all your wedding presents. I figured you wouldn't want to see them. I also hid all the pictures of TJ, not that there were many." That was true, I hadn't had a lot of them up. Come to think of it, I didn't have a lot of pictures of myself with TJ, not even on my phone. We'd just never taken that many. The only ones I could remember had been sent to me by other people.

"I can delete the ones off your phone if you want." She still had my phone.

"No, I can do that." I'd probably throw up while doing it, but it was all part of the process. I wondered if he'd sent me any further messages.

I also still needed to draft a message to the other girl.

We made it back to my place in the early afternoon and I was ready to go to sleep again, but Tessa had gotten some coffee brandy, and I figured that had to have some caffeine in it. I sat down at my little kitchen table and watched as Tessa pulled out some glasses.

"Okay, I think we're supposed to mix it with milk, or Moxie soda, but that's not happening." Tessa looked up from her phone and made a gagging noise. Moxie was supposed to be the Coke or Pepsi of Maine, but neither of us was a big fan.

"Milk's fine." Tessa assembled drinks and I sucked one back and slammed the glass down.

"Give me a second to catch up," Tessa said, trying to chug the glass and then choking. She got the glass down but made a face. "Ugh, too much milk in that one. Do you have any chocolate syrup or anything?" I happened to have some in the fridge, so she pulled that out, and then went to the freezer for some ice cream.

"Oh shit, let's do this."

A few minutes later she handed me a boozy frappe. That was much harder to down than when she'd just mixed it with milk, but maybe that was a good thing.

"Oh, this is good. I'm going to get wasted." Tessa sang the last word as she sucked the frappe through a straw.

"Not if I get wasted first," I said. Tessa was adorable when she had too much to drink. She got flirty and handsy and loved literally everyone. If she had too much, she would start crying about random things, like thinking about butterflies being hit by cars.

In contrast, I was all over the place, and could get, as Tessa put it "broody." Honestly, I was kind of hoping to drink until I forgot about TJ for a little while. I'd never been truly drunk before, I liked control for too much, so why not go for it now?

Both of us finished our frappes, and then Tessa made more.

"Come on, let's go sit on the couch. I just want to snuggle with a blanket." There she was. It did not take much for Tessa to start being silly.

"Sure," I said, and we took our third rounds to the living room. I sat on the couch and Tessa draped herself across my lap, covering us with a crocheted blanket one of her aunts had made.

"Play with my hairrrrr," she whined. I held my drink with one hand and ran my fingers through her hair with the other as she hummed softly. My body was warm and my thoughts rolled softly, like gentle waves.

"This is nice," I said, closing my eyes and resting my head on the back of the couch. I went slower with my third drink, and by the time the glass was empty, I was feeling pleasantly tipsy.

Tessa sighed happily and snuggled closer to me. Her weight was warm and cozy, even though I had started to sweat.

"I'm glad you're not getting married," she said, and I thought that I'd misheard her.

"You're glad that my fuck of a fiancé cheated on me?"

She turned so she was on her back looking up at me.

"No. I'm not glad about that at all. But I'm glad you found out now and not after you tied yourself to him and moved in and everything." That was a good point I hadn't thought of.

"I wonder why I wasn't enough," I said, voicing one of the thoughts that kept spinning over and over in my head.

"Hey, don't you dare think that this has anything to do with you. TJ is lower than the mold on a rotting dildo covered in shit." The more she drank, the more colorful her language got, and I couldn't help but laugh at that one.

Tessa touched my face and stared into my eyes.

"You're enough, Ford. You're everything." I looked down at her and I felt even warmer as something fluttered in my chest. TJ may not have loved me, but Tessa did. At least I had that. I had her, and she wasn't going anywhere.

"Thanks. I don't feel like that right now," I said.

"I know. But you will. You'll get through this because you're strong and you're amazing and I know you're going to find someone who's worthy of you." I snorted.

"You don't think any guy is worthy of me."

There was chocolate on her mouth, and I thought about wiping it away, but I didn't. "Well, that's because no guy is."

She was impossible. "Tessa!"

"I'm sorry, it's true!" Another thing that happened when Tessa drank was that she got louder and louder. They could probably hear her in the coffee shop downstairs.

"I need another drink. Move, please." She rolled off me

and I got to my feet, a little unsteady. Not quite at "the floor is liquid" stage, but I was on my way. Everything was sloshy.

"How much of this do you put in?" I called to Tessa as I started pouring the brandy in the blender.

"Enough," was the answer.

"Works for me."

SEVERAL HOURS later I was laughing my ass off, but I couldn't remember why. Tessa was singing, and we were both sitting on the floor. We'd given up on the frappes and were just drinking right from the bottle, passing it back and forth.

Someone's phone had been going off, but we'd both been ignoring it.

"Shut uppppp," Tessa said, pulling out said phone and squinting at it. "Shit, my parents are being annoying." Instead of trying to type out a message, she used speech to text and sent a reply.

I curled up on the floor and sighed.

"I hate him. He was supposed to be my husband. I was supposed to have a husband. Now I have to find a new husband," I moaned. "How do you find a husband?"

"I don't know, Gus found me." Tessa started giggling as if that was the funniest thing in the world, and I laughed with her because for some reason it was.

"I have to have a husband, Cin. You're supposed to have a husband." That had always been my goal. I wanted to be married by twenty-five, and be having children by twenty-seven. I'd even written an essay on it and fourth grade and made vision boards and shit. That was my life, that was my path, and TJ had fucked the whole thing up.

"You can't have my husband. He's mine," she said.

"I don't want yours. But I need my own. Husband! Where is my husband?" I started yelling and then laughed again.

"Husbanddddddddd," Tessa sang over and over. She rolled into me and we tangled together, laughing our asses off.

"Tired now," I said. "Bedtime."

"Sleep sleeps," she said. "Night night."

We curled together on the floor and that was the last thing I remembered, falling asleep with Tessa's hair in my face. It smelled like coconut lime.

Chapter Five

TESSA

I woke up on Monty's floor with the worst fucking hangover of my entire life. I'd also never had to pee so bad.

Somehow, I made it to the bathroom without hurling or falling or injuring myself, but it was close.

When I made it back to the living room, Monty was moaning as well.

"Why did we sleep on the floor?" I asked in a whisper.

"Too loud," she said, and then her eyes flew wide. She was going to hurl, so I grabbed the closest trash can and held it in front of her face just in time.

Somehow I was able to keep myself from joining her as her stomach tried to turn itself inside out to rid her body of the alcohol we'd consumed.

I didn't know if I'd ever felt so completely awful before. It had been fun at the time, but now I had major regrets.

The two of us were a sorry sight for a while. We both ended up having to call in sick again, and I didn't have to fake anything when I said I had a stomach bug. I also sent messages to my parents, but they didn't seem too concerned. I mean, they did deal with my brothers before they got to me, so by the time I came along, they'd been through pretty much everything. I was a breeze in comparison.

Monty and I took turns puking and nursing each other and by the afternoon, we were starting to see the light at the end of the hangover tunnel.

I still had her phone, and she had a massive amount of messages from TJ and her parents. Somehow, they must have found out. I didn't know who had told them, but it was only a matter of time before the whole damn town found out, and she had to deal with the gossip monsters. This was fresh, dramatic meat and they were always hungry. I was ready to put on my fucking armor and defend her to the end from them trying to devour her.

She was hurting enough, and those fuckers didn't need to add to it.

"I need to deal with the wedding stuff," she said, a cold cloth on her forehead as she sprawled on the couch.

"Tell me who you need to contact. I can pretend to be you." She listed it off, and I used her phone to start sending messages. I also put in asks for refunds, even though I knew what the answers were probably going to be. I didn't give details, just that the wedding was off, and could they see it in their hearts to grant even a partial refund?

Even though it was a small wedding, I spent a long time going back and forth with the various vendors. There really should be some kind of app for this so you could write one message and it would go to everyone and deal with the responses. Maybe I'd create it.

"Can I have some privacy?" Monty asked when she decided it was time to call her parents.

"Yeah, I should probably like, go home anyway." She'd been progressively pulling away, and I knew Monty enough to know that she needed some space. I didn't think she was in danger of being alone, so I gave her a hug and made sure to take the rest of the alcohol with me when I left so she wouldn't get any other ideas about getting drunk again.

"How is she?" Mom asked when I walked through the door. She was a secretary at the local high school, and my dad managed the hardware store, so she was always the first one home.

"I mean, we got really drunk on coffee brandy and cancelled all her wedding shit, so I think she's okay? I also have all her wedding gifts in the trunk of my car so she doesn't have to see them."

Mom crossed her arms and tsked. "I can't believe he did that to her. What a fucker. I swear, if I see his mother, I'm going to give her a piece of my mind for raising a piece of shit." I didn't doubt it. And if she saw TJ, I could imagine the words she'd have for him too.

"Can you not, until I talk to Ford about it? I don't think she wants her best friend's mom to do that. I think she just wants it to go away right now."

Mom glowered, and I almost wanted to run away as if I'd done something wrong. She hadn't raised three men to adulthood without mastering being utterly terrifying with just one look.

"I can respect that. But just say the word and he's done. Done."

"I'm sure she'll appreciate that."

I put a hand to my pounding head and then flopped over on the couch. I'd been taking care of Monty and it had taken a toll.

"You okay?" Mom put her hand on my forehead, as moms were wont to do.

"Just tired. I couldn't sleep at all because I was worried she was going to wake up and now I'm just exhausted." She stroked my hair and kissed my forehead.

"You're a good friend, Tessa. I'm so proud of the way you care for Monty." That made my heart swell a little bit. "How about some comfort food?"

"That sounds great." I closed my eyes and rested my head back on the couch cushions.

Sure, I was a grown-ass woman, but I still loved when my mom made me a grilled cheese sandwich on sourdough and a bowl of canned tomato soup with oyster crackers on top and a glass of iced tea. Pretty much the perfect lunch combination.

"Thanks, Mom. This is perfect."

I had a little more energy after I ate, but I still needed sleep, so I took a nap and when I woke up, Dad was home and watching the news from his recliner.

"Hey," I said, my voice scratchy. It must be late. I shouldn't have slept so long. Oops.

"Hey, how are you doing? I heard about Tessa, that's terrible." I sat up and waited for a little dizzy spell to pass.

"Just tired. I should check on her." I grabbed my phone from the coffee table, and I had a message from Monty, asking how I was doing.

Fine, just took a nap. You?

I mean, she was one the one whose life had kind of gotten blown up.

IDK anymore. I slept a little. Not sure what I'm supposed to do now. Don't want to see anyone, but I don't want to be alone.

That was a little worrying.

Come over. My parents won't bug you. Stay over and then you won't have to be alone.

If she didn't want to, I'd go back over to her place and stay over again. I didn't even care if I missed another day of work or got fired. I wouldn't even need to spin a sob story about why I'd missed so many days.

If that's okay Monty said, as if my parents wouldn't take her in in a heartbeat.

Get here when you can I responded.

"Ford's coming over. She said she didn't want to be alone, but she probably doesn't want to talk about it, so can you both be cool?" I said and my parents shared a look.

"We'll behave," Dad said.

"Does she want anything? I'm happy to make dinner or heat up some leftovers." There was no shortage of leftovers in the O'Connell house. My parents had gotten used to feeding three teen boys and hadn't lost the habit of making way too much in anticipation that someone would come by and devour whatever it was.

"I'll ask when she gets here."

I didn't know why I was fretting about Monty getting to the house, but she didn't show up until nearly an hour later, and when she walked through the door her hair was still wet from the shower and, honestly, she looked like shit. Her skin was too pale, except for the red blotchy patches under her eyes and on her cheeks. The puffiness around her eyes hadn't gone down at all. Monty always dressed carefully, but the outfit she had on was something I'd never even seen before: sweatpants that had enormous holes and a faded t-shirt from a camp we'd attended when we were ten that I didn't even know she had anymore. On her feet were two different socks. She hadn't even brought shoes.

"Oh, Ford," I said, holding my arms open. She stumbled into them and I pulled her inside.

~

MONTY STAYED with me for nearly a week. I woke her up and made her eat breakfast and shower and go to work. She did a lot of staring at walls and not a lot of talking, but we got over the initial hump of grief. Then it got out (I didn't know how) about her and TJ, and then I spent my time following her around and hovering whenever she was near anyone else in case they asked her about it or gave her pitying looks. Those came, as did the whispers. Honestly, I didn't listen to a lot of the gossip because that shit didn't matter, but I heard it nonetheless.

Monty was stoic through it all, but I heard her crying the guest room at night sometimes. I tried to comfort her, but she told me that she had to deal with it alone, so I just gave her a hug and went back to bed to worry about her.

The boxes she'd taken to TJ's showed up on her steps, and he didn't try to contact her further. She did end up writing a message to the other girl, but she didn't hear anything back. That was probably for the best.

In the second week after everything, she started looking better and I even caught what I thought might be a smile or two. Always focused, she threw herself into work, volunteering for way too many things and meetings and committees to fill up her time, but I didn't blame her.

Her parents finding out was the roughest part. There was a lot of screaming and crying on the part of her mother and a lot of disappointed words from her dad. As if she'd been the one who'd done wrong. I'd never really gotten along with them, and they'd been pretty absent for most of her life. I would never, ever have said this to her, but they were the kind of people who got pressured into having kids because it was supposedly the right thing to do, but probably shouldn't have.

I was so glad when she got to get away from them when she went to college and got her own place. They pretty much sucked.

Every night she stayed with us, I would wake up and creep to the guest room and check on her. I couldn't help myself. I had to make sure that she was okay. I think she was beginning to get annoyed with me when I kept texting her during work to check in. Not to mention all the times I brought her coffee and food to make sure she ate.

One week before her wedding was supposed to happen, there was a knock at my bedroom door in the middle of the night. I shot out of bed, fumbling with my covers.

"Come in," I thought I said, but it might have been gibberish because I was still half asleep.

"Hey," Monty said in a soft voice. I was instantly alert.

"You okay?" I reached out to her and she sat on my bed. She didn't look like she'd been sleeping.

"Yeah, I was thinking. My honeymoon was all paid for. Hotel and everything. I can't get the money back for TJ's ticket," she didn't even flinch when she said his name, "but I could get one for you. We could go together. Get out of town for a week. What do you think?"

"Fuck yeah, I'm in." I didn't need to know anything else. I'd forgotten even where she was going, because I hadn't wanted to put any thought about Monty leaving me and going off with him. Now that wasn't happening, I was all too thrilled to take his place, so to speak.

"It'll be a bestfriendimoon," I said, pulling the term out of my ass on the spot.

"Sure, why not," she said, and yawned. "I hoped you were going to be in. Since I can't do much else with any of the left-over shit." I'd helped her return the gifts to the senders. I told her she could keep them, but she wanted to stick to accepted etiquette. She could heal and grieve in whatever way worked for her. Monty had also gotten money as gifts and she had plans to donate what she didn't return to charity, which I also had questions about, but I did my best friend thing and didn't make any comments.

"Okay, I should go back to bed." Part of me wanted to reach out and stop her. To pull her into bed with me like we had when we were kids and whispering secrets late into the night under the covers, listening for my mom's footsteps in the hallway.

I didn't ask her to stay, because why would I? We'd been a lot smaller when we'd shared this bed and there wasn't a reason to do that now. She had a huge bed in the guest room, all to herself.

I swallowed the question as she stood up and headed toward the door.

"Night, Ford," I said.

"Night, Cin." She closed the door and I breathed for a second. Her scent was still in the air for a few moments, but she wasn't here anymore.

THE NEXT DAY I was tweaking a display of Maine-centric gifts when someone tapped me on the shoulder. I jumped and turned around to curse the person out and found Monty holding a frozen coffee out to me.

"Don't do that, Ford. I might have punched you."

She handed me the coffee with a raised eyebrow. "So you're telling me that you would punch a customer who tapped you on the shoulder?"

I sucked on the icy drink. "Probably not."

"Is there one of those for me?" Ron said, coming over to us.

"Sorry, next time," Monty said, giving him a quick hug. He and Bill adored her and were always saying that she should take over the shop when they retired.

"Where's Bill?" Monty asked. You almost never saw Ron, who wasn't much taller than me, without his hulking husband Bill, who had never met a flannel shirt he didn't like. Bill always looked like he should be out in a remote cabin wrestling bears and chopping wood, not carefully arranging antique books under glass with white gloves like he did every week. He had a degree in archival science and had worked for several museums before meeting Ron and moving to Maine and starting the shop. He didn't say much, but whatever he did say was always worth listening to.

"Out hunting treasures," Ron said with a fond smile. Bill traveled all around, searching for rare and hard-to-find books, and rescuing some from people who weren't sure how to care of them. He and Ron often taught bookbinding classes in the evenings as well.

"He has my list?" Monty said, and Ron patted her arm.

"He has your list."

Monty had a list of rare books that she would give one of her arms to have, and Bill always made sure to see if he could find them for her. They had a cute relationship and were both in charge of the local book club that met at the library once a month.

"How are you doing?" Ron asked, concern in his eyes. I felt a bolt of frustration for Monty, because even though the question was well-meaning, it just brought all that pain to the surface.

"I'm doing well," she said, which was her patented response. "Thank you for asking." Monty plastered a serene smile on her face and made eye contact with me.

"Can we talk for a second?"

"Yeah, absolutely. You can have all my seconds."

Ron rolled his eyes. "Just don't take too many and ignore the customers looking for 'that blue book.'" That made all of us laugh because we'd all experienced a customer who was looking for a book, but the only detail they knew about it was the color of the cover and no other identifying details.

Monty and I ducked over to a more-deserted part of the store and I leaned against a shelf.

"What's up?"

"I'm going back to my apartment tonight. I think it's time. You and your parents have been seriously the best, but I need to start getting back to something that's like normal. I need to figure out how to live my life on my own again."

Everything in me knew she was right, knew this was right. Of course she couldn't just crash in the guest room forever. That didn't stop me from wanting to fucking breakdown right next to a cookbook full of kale recipes.

"You should get a cat," I said, when I trusted myself to be able to speak and not start crying and begging her to stay.

"From the cat sanctuary? Maybe I will after we get back from our trip."

"Our bestfriendimoon," I corrected.

She huffed out something that might be a laugh. "You know I'm not calling it that."

"You'll come around to my way of thinking. You always do."

"We'll see," she said. "I've got to get back to work."

"Thanks for the coffee," I said, sucking the last of the watery remnants from the bottom of the cup.

"You're welcome. I won't see you tonight, I guess. But I'll see you tomorrow?"

I chewed on the straw. "Sure, sounds good."

She left and I collapsed against the shelf, fighting the urge to cry as if I was never going to see her again. Being a best friend made me really dramatic, apparently.

I needed to get my shit together.

Chapter Six

MONTY

It was strange being back at my place. Tessa was right, I did need something else to be here with me. In the few weeks I'd been staying with her family, I'd gotten out of the habit of being alone. The silence didn't give me solace. It chafed against my skin like sandpaper, making me feel itchy and uncomfortable. I kept wandering around, rearranging things, including my furniture. Since my place was so small, there weren't a whole lot of configurations that would work with what I had, so I started thinking about getting some new things. I'd been planning on doing that anyway, so why not? At least this time I could pick everything out myself.

The initial shock of everything had worn off and I realized one harsh truth: I didn't miss TJ. Sure, I thought about him, but the more days that passed, the less I thought about him, and the less I even remembered about him. When was the last time we had kissed? What color were his eyes, exactly? Was he funny? I didn't know, and that was disturbing.

In the middle of the night, when I couldn't sleep, one question ran through my mind, as if it was on repeat: why were you with him?

Why, indeed? To answer that question, I went back to the beginning. He'd asked me out, I'd said yes and then…that was it. He was my boyfriend and then my fiancé. He was the guy. That was how it worked. You graduated, you got a job, you got a guy, you got married, you had kids. That was the plan, that was the dream, that was everything I'd ever wanted.

Right?

But was he really what I wanted? I didn't have an answer for that.

If it wasn't TJ, who was it? Honestly, the idea of meeting someone new and trying to date made me sick to my stomach. I'd even scanned online dating sites, because who was I going to meet here that I didn't already know? None of the guys around here was even remotely appealing.

So I went back to thinking about getting a cat until I was exhausted enough to fall asleep.

"HI, I'm hoping you can help me," someone said, as I was dusting off the computers while monitoring a few kids who were looking things up online and giggling. The library had lots of internet filters, but kids could pretty much hack through anything these days.

I turned around and found a girl so beautiful I couldn't speak for a second. One hand gripped the edge of the table for balance.

"Sure," I said, even though I had no idea what she'd just said. I'd been stunned by her blonde halo of curls and the kinds of cheekbones that could cut glass. If you would have told me she was a Viking princess that had the powers of time-travel, I wouldn't have questioned it.

"Sorry, I'm just visiting, but I was wondering if you could tell me where a good place to get some lobster might be? I was driving by and thought someone here would know."

I nodded, even though it took me a few moments to process all of the words she'd said. People came in here all the time asking for directions, for recommendations, and sometimes for really random things. The library was kind of a catch-all around here for people looking for answers. To be honest, I kind of loved being a keeper of information. It made me feel powerful in an unpredictable world.

"Oh, yeah, you should definitely go to Lenny's Lobster Shack. It's actually a food truck that's parked near the beach, but those are the best around. If you're looking for more of a restaurant, sit-down place, go to Christine's. They also have amazing sangria." I clamped my mouth shut so I didn't ramble on. There was something about beautiful women that made it hard for me to speak normally. They were just so intimidating.

"Oh, the sangria sounds dangerous. I'll have to be careful and not have too many." I blinked at her and then belatedly laughed. She had to be a model or something. The way she carried herself on those heels was so natural, I felt like a peasant in comparison. As we said in Maine, she *definitely* wasn't from around here.

"Yeah, it's great," I said to fill the silence. "Uh, how long are you in town?"

"Just a few days. I'm visiting a friend. Are you from here?" Oh, we were having a conversation now and I was sweating, even in the air conditioning.

"Yeah, born and raised. I left for college, but I moved back. I can't imagine living anywhere else." The teenagers were giggling over something that probably had to do with butts and I needed to go intervene, but I couldn't pull myself away from this beautiful creature.

"I can see why, it's so lovely here." Her phone made a noise and she looked down at an incoming message. "That's my friend, I'm supposed to go meet her. Thanks so much for your help…" she trailed off, waiting for me to say my name.

"Monty," I said, suddenly self-conscious about my name. Why, oh why, had my parents named me Montgomery? Did they have to use *that* family name?

"Monty? That's cute. I'm Isadora." Even her name was impossibly gorgeous and out of my league. "So nice to meet you, Monty. I hope we run into each other again."

Against my will, my face went completely and totally red and I mumbled some sort of goodbye before she left and then I had to get myself together and go and see what the teens were up to.

"HEY, Gus and I are at the beach. You should come over and get some ice cream with us," Tessa said when she called me after work. That sounded kind of perfect, so I packed up my stuff, said bye to everyone, and drove the short distance to the beach.

I waved my pass at the bored dude sitting at the ticket booth and shaded my eyes to find Tessa and Gus. The place wasn't as crowded as it would have been at the height of the day, so it wasn't hard to slip off my shoes and walk toward where they'd crashed on the blanket Tessa kept in the trunk of her car for times exactly like this.

"Hey," I said. Tessa beamed at me and I sat down next to her as Gus said hello. The three of us had been hanging out together for so long that I often forgot they were actually engaged and getting married. Unlike me.

My engagement ring had always thrown me off, but now that it was gone from my finger, I almost missed it. Almost.

"You doing good?" Gus asked, pulling a can out of a cooler

and passing it to me. The beach didn't technically allow alcohol, but it wasn't like anyone was going to arrest us for violating the rules. Plus, Tessa had worked here a few summers in high school and knew everyone who worked here so she could talk her way out of being in trouble.

"I guess," I said, popping the can and taking a sip. I wasn't a beer person, but when in Rome.

"I know I've said it before, but I'm really sorry, Monty."

"Thanks, Gus." He gave me a hug and I sighed. Gus was a great guy, honestly. He was so steady and solid and Tessa needed someone like that in her life.

"So, we were talking about something and I need your input, Ford," Tessa said, leaning back on her elbows and turning her face up.

"What's that?" I sipped my beer and then pushed it into the sand so it didn't tip over.

"Milk vs. no milk in cereal. Discuss."

"Well, on the one hand, you have milk, which makes the cereal less dry, and you get cereal milk as a treat at the end. Downside is that, depending on the cereal, it can get soggy and there's no coming back from that. Upside of no milk is no dilution or sogginess, but given the right cereal, you might end up with your mouth bleeding."

Tessa grinned at Gus in triumph. "See?"

"Why, what did you say?" I asked him.

"I don't like my cereal wet. That's disgusting."

"Yeah, and who is the one who bitches about your mouth being sore?" Tessa shot back and I closed my eyes and lay back on the blanket, listening to them bicker. It was never about anything serious, and I was so used to it, I would have been thrown off if they weren't sniping at each other over something as inconsequential as cereal.

The next thing I knew, Tessa was rousing me and the sun had dipped lower in the sky, setting us up for what looked to be a brilliant sunset. Most of the people had left, and there were just a few people walking their dogs or sitting in the sand.

"What did I miss?" I asked, rubbing my eyes.

"Nothing. Gus is just mad that he's not coming on the trip with us." Gus made a sputtering sound.

"That's not true. I think it's great that you're going together. Why would I be mad?"

Tessa bumped his shoulder with hers and grinned. "You know I'm just giving you a hard time."

Did Gus want to come? I mean, I guess that would be fine, but it would be a little weird. Sure, we'd gone on trips together, but this was a whole week, and I'd already started looking at places in Savannah that Tessa would want to go. She didn't know that she'd be coming with me on several historical tours, but we'd cross that bridge when we got there.

"I'm starving," Tessa said. "Dinner?" She looked at Gus.

"Yeah, you want to stop and grab a pizza?"

I looked out at the ocean as they argued about what kind of pizza to get. That argument always ended the same: half pepperoni and olive, half green pepper and mushroom. No idea why they fought to begin with, since that's what they always ordered.

There was a chicken defrosting on my counter at home. The plan was to bake it in the oven, but with the impromptu nap I'd taken, I didn't have the energy anymore.

"You want to come over? We'll get you your own spinach and artichoke," Tessa said.

"No, that's fine. I have something in the crockpot," I lied.

"Okay," she said, and let Gus help her to her feet. I also got up and helped them pack up the blanket and everything else.

"Thanks for this. I needed a break from everything," I said.

"Anytime. What are friends for?" Gus said, and gave me a hug. The three of us hadn't hung out as a trio in a long time, and I probably needed to work on that. I guess when they'd gotten engaged I'd pulled back on being with them because I thought they wanted privacy, but they'd never asked for that. Maybe I needed to reconnect with them now that I wasn't going to be spending time with TJ. The future stretched out in front of me and I just wanted to close my eyes and sleep through it.

"Call me later?" Tessa said, brushing her hand on my shoulder to get rid of some sand.

"Yeah, I will."

She looked like she was going to say something else, but instead wrapped her arms around me. I melted into her and sighed.

"Thanks for being my best friend," she said, and I had to choke down some tears. I wasn't going to cry. I was so fucking sick of crying.

"There's nothing to thank me for." She gave me one last squeeze and let go. The three of us walked to our vehicles and I waved goodbye as Tessa got in Gus's Jeep.

Alone again.

"YOU'D BETTER BE PACKING," I said a few days later, the night before we were due to fly to Savannah.

"Uhhhh, yeah. I'm packing," Tessa said.

"So you're telling me if I suddenly gained the ability to teleport that I would find you putting clothes and other items into a suitcase right now?"

There was a rustling sound.

"Yes, definitely."

"Tessa."

"I'm waiting for the dryer to finish! I'm doing it! You're worse than my mom, Jesus." More rustling and some cursing.

"Please, just get your stuff packed sooner rather than later.

I am not doing that thing where we have to rush through security and run to the gate."

Tessa snorted. "Ford, it takes like two seconds to run from one end of the airport to the other. This is Portland, Maine, not LaGuardia."

That was true, but I still didn't want to add any extra stress on the trip. I almost wished we were driving instead of flying, because there was so much that could go wrong when planes were involved.

"Please, Cin. This isn't easy for me, can you not?"

She sighed. "Shit. I'm sorry. I'm being a jerk. Yeah, I'm going to pack right now, as soon as my stuff comes out of the dryer. I'll even send you a picture as proof. You know we don't have to go."

I looked at my already packed suitcase. "No, I want to do this. I need to do this." My need to get away from this town, away from the memories and gossip it brought had grown by the day and I was just done. It was time for something new, someplace new, even if it was just for a week. I needed to breathe new air and see new people.

"I'm good, I promise."

"Okay. I'll get my shit together and see you tomorrow at the asscrack of dawn."

"Cute, I'll see you tomorrow."

She signed off with a grumbling noise and I did get a picture of a suitcase a few hours later as I was trying to trick myself into going to sleep early so I wasn't dragging tomorrow. It took an hour and a half to get to the airport, and we needed time to go through security, so leaving early enough to make our flight was crucial.

Almost time for bestfriendimoon.

Chapter Seven

TESSA

"See? I told you we were going to be fine," I said through a yawn as we waited in the uncomfortable airport chairs. I'd propped my feet up on my luggage, and my foot kept falling asleep. There were only a few other people at our gate, and our flight wasn't for another hour. I was so fucking tired already and I needed to catch some sleep on the plane so I'd be ready for fun when we got to Savannah.

Monty had been on her phone nearly the whole time and I kept trying to engage her in conversation, but I could tell she wanted to be left alone, so I tried to amuse myself by just staring at everyone else. I couldn't lie, I would hang out in this airport all day watching everyone else. What a fascinating place.

Most of the time I was too broke for much travel, so this was something special and I was going to make the most of it, at least, after I'd had a nap.

"Mmmm," Monty said, scrolling mindlessly through her phone. Giving up, I put on my headphones and listened to podcasts until it was finally, *finally* time to board the flight.

By some miracle, Monty and I had managed to get seats together on the tiny plane. I didn't know what I would have done if we hadn't been next to each other.

Once we got seated, I got myself as comfortable as I could be in the window seat, but there just wasn't a whole lot of wiggle room. Monty was still on her phone, but I could see one of her eyes twitching, which definitely meant she was freaking out a little.

"We'll be there in no time," I said, squeezing her arm clamped on the armrest.

"Sure," she said, not looking up from her phone. I didn't think she even knew what she was looking at anymore.

"Lay back and put your headphones on. You've seen the safety demo before." She finally looked up and met me with wild eyes. Yup, she was panicking.

"Here," I said, rummaging through my purse. I pulled out an eye mask I'd been intending to use myself, but I could sacrifice it for a good cause. Monty put the mask on, her headphones on her ears, and lay her head back. No more doomscrolling. I sat back in my seat and after a few moments, rested my head on her shoulder. Ahhhh, perfect. I snuggled into her and closed my eyes.

I woke up a little as the plane took off, and then it was naptime until Monty was gently shaking me.

"Whaa?" I said, immediately regretting being awake. My body was crunched like a pretzel and I had to pee so bad I thought I was going to need a new pair of jeans.

"We're here," she said, and she looked a little less twitchy than when we took off.

"Did you sleep any?" I asked.

"No, but you did. Bitch."

I laughed through a yawn and looked around as we waited to deplane. From there it was a mission to get our luggage from the overhead and then get in a car to take us to the hotel.

"It's hot as Satan's butthole," I said, regretting wearing said jeans. I hadn't thought about that when we'd left Maine, but I probably should have.

"I think I told you to wear something looser," Monty said as we drove away from the airport and got on the highway.

"Well, that doesn't help me now, does it?" I grumbled. At least the car had air conditioning, and the hotel would too. The first thing I needed to do was take a shower and change. I hoped Monty would get in a short nap before forcing us to partake in some sort of activity. I knew she had an itinerary on her phone that she'd been trying to hide from me.

It was safe to say that Savannah was different than Maine, and not just the heat. So many historic homes and plaques and statues. And the trees, I couldn't get over them. They were huge and had these heavy tendrils hanging down everywhere. I just wanted to sit under one and drink a sweet tea or something.

Monty checked us in and the person at the desk looked at her account and then beamed at her.

"Congratulations, Mrs. Murray, we're so happy to have you here." The blood drained from Monty's face and I grabbed onto her so her legs didn't give out.

"Uh, yeah, do whatever you need to do in the computer to get rid of that info," I said to the confused front desk person, and then explained the situation in hushed tones.

"Oh, I'm so sorry. I'll get that updated right away." Monty started making a weird gasping noise as the front desk person clacked on the keyboard to remove mentions of Monty being married.

"Ford, are you okay?" I looked into her face and I saw tears starting to run down her cheeks. Shit, this had been a bad idea.

"Here are your room keys, and I'm sending up a complimentary bottle of champagne." It was the least they could do.

"Sounds good," I said, taking the room keys, Monty's arm,

and somehow getting the luggage on a cart so we could go up to our room.

Monty started to get her bearings in the elevator, but I still wanted her to lay down for a little while, or maybe take a soak in the tub or something. I'd have to check out what they had for room service options.

After a little fumbling, I got us through the door and then tried to block the view from Monty.

"Go into the bathroom," I told her.

"Why?" She tried to shove past me.

"Just go in the damn bathroom for a few seconds, Ford." Monty glared at me, but stepped into the bathroom and shut the door. I rushed to the bed, which was covered in a heart made from fake rose petals. I brushed them onto the floor and shoved as many of them as I could under the bed. There wasn't anything else wedding related, so that was good.

"Can I come out now?" Monty called from the bathroom, clearly irritated.

"Yes, you're good."

"Oh," she said, looking at the bed, that was a little rumpled from my efforts to remove the petals. "I forgot there's only one bed."

"Right." That hadn't even occurred to me at first, but it was a big bed. We could share it. No big deal. "I mean, we've shared a bed how many times before?"

"Good point," she said, and then she flopped down on her back on the bed.

"Do you need anything?" I found some bottles of water in the fridge and handed her one. The room was beautiful, and even had a little balcony I could see us having breakfast on in the mornings in fluffy robes like fancy people. Hopefully I could make room for that in her itinerary. I really needed to get my hands on her phone so I could find it and see what I was in for.

"A new life?" she said, shutting her eyes and throwing her arm over her face.

"Sorry, I'm fresh out, but how about a snack?" I found the room service menu but was interrupted by a knock on the door. A waiter had a try with an ice bucket and two glasses, as well as a tray of chocolate strawberries. As if the hotel had read my mind.

"Wow, thank you so much," I said, and gave the guy a generous tip.

"Compliments of the front desk," he said with an awkward little bow.

I wheeled the cart into the room.

"Come have a glass of bubbly with me," I said, and Monty sat up. I opened the bottle and poured her a glass. I set the tray of strawberries on the bed and plunked down next to her.

"To the bestfriendimoon," I said, holding my glass out. She clinked hers against mine and then downed the whole thing in one go.

This was going to be an interesting week.

I CHECKED in with my parents, and after gulping two glasses of champagne and munching a few strawberries, Monty crashed out on the bed. I was relieved, so I stepped out on the balcony to enjoy the view and not disturb her nap.

I hung up after giving them the rundown of the flight and the hotel and how Monty was doing (I glossed over a lot and said she was doing fine), I sat on the chair and sipped the rest of the bottle of water. Not too shabby. I knew that this trip was making a rainbow from the absolute shittiest storm possible, but I had one goal for this trip: to force Monty to have some damn fun. I didn't care what I had to do to make that happen.

She might have made plans, but I had a few tricks up my sleeve too, and she wasn't going to know what hit her.

~

IT WAS NEARLY time for dinner when Monty woke up. Her eyes were puffy, but she looked a little less grim than she had when we'd first arrived.

"Good evening, sunshine. How was your nap?"

She looked around the room and had such a confused expression on her face that I couldn't handle it.

"What time is it?" she croaked, running a hand through her hair. She'd slept with it down, so it was just all over the place. Monty normally braided her hair at night since it was so long and got so chaotic if she didn't.

"Almost six-thirty. Are you hungry?"

She sat up and leaned against the pillows.

"Just give me a few minutes to get my bearings. I think I might want a shower first, even if we don't go anywhere."

I turned on the TV and flipped around while she hopped in the shower and changed her clothes. When she came back into the room, she looked a lot fresher, and I could tell her mood was better.

"We could go down to the restaurant here, if you didn't want to venture anywhere else." I'd already changed from the clothes I'd had on earlier, so I was good to go.

"Sounds good." I watched as she braided her damp hair without thought and spun it into a perfect loose bun on the back of her head. Her dress fluttered in the air conditioning as she slipped her sandals on.

"It's the first dinner of bestfriendimoon. Let's do this," I said, linking her arm with mine.

"You're going to make bestfriendimoon into a whole big

thing, aren't you?" she said, giving me side-eye as we walked down the hallway toward the elevator.

"There might be t-shirts and other memorabilia," I said, and her eyes went wide.

"Please don't say that Donny made shirts." My brother Donny was an incredible artist and enjoyed designing t-shirts and other promotional items as a hobby. He'd done the sign for the antique store, and every year for Pride he made new shirts for the whole family that we wore at the parade.

"I have no idea what you're talking about," I said, and she yanked on my arm so I'd stop walking.

"I'm not wearing matching t-shirts." She crossed her arms and leaned on one hip.

"We'll see about that," I said, walking and hitting the down button on the elevator.

"I'm not wearing matching shirts," she said through clenched teeth as we got on the elevator.

"We'll see," I said.

Monty argued with me all the way down the elevator, and it was a relief to see her so feisty.

The restaurant inside the hotel was actually pretty nice, with lovely antique chandeliers casting warm light, and lots of leather chairs, and a really cool bar.

We got a table and glanced at the menus.

"So, what else do you want to do this evening? Just chill? I have face masks and shit." It had required a miracle to get all of the supplies to make this the bestfriendimoon, but somehow I'd done it. I was so impressed with myself.

"Could we just maybe take a walk? Just wander around?"

Honestly, that sounded amazing. We could do that and also do the other fun things I had in my suitcase of fun.

"I love it, perfect idea."

Dinner was incredible: fried chicken for both of us, mac

and cheese, salads, and fried Oreos for dessert. I opted for iced tea instead of booze for some balance. Plus, if I had any alcohol with all that food, I might have fallen asleep under the table.

"Maybe a walk was a bad idea," Monty said as she sat back, both hands on her stomach. She groaned and rubbed her belly.

"Let's sit here for a few minutes and let everything settle. Okay, what do you think their deal is?" I nodded toward a man and a woman at another table. Both were dressed for a date night, but you never knew.

"It's not awkward enough for a date. And there's no chemistry. I'm guessing some sort of work thing. And look how he's talking and talking and talking and she's doing the 'politely interested' thing." She was right.

"Okay, second question: what do they do for a living?"

Monty studied the people, her head tilted just slightly to the side. I hadn't had any alcohol, but my skin was warm, and I kept getting distracted by the shine on her hair from the chandeliers. Sometimes I envied her hair and thought about growing mine out, but I couldn't stand having hair on the back of my neck, so that was a no go. Undercut was my comfort zone.

Plus, I wasn't pretty like Monty. No one was pretty like Monty.

"Real estate," she said with confidence.

"I'm voting for lawyers." They had that lawyer look. We'd never find out the real story, but it was fun to speculate. The two of us went from table to table, making increasingly ridiculous suggestions.

"You ready?" I asked, and she nodded.

"Just a short walk. My tired is catching up with me," she said as we got up from the table. A group had come in and taken over the bar and they were loud as hell. I wasn't old by any means, but did they have to be like that? Have some decorum and use your inside voice.

The air was thick with moisture when we walked outside.

"Dear god, how do people live like this," I said, my skin instantly breaking out in a sweat. It was too late for it to be so hot.

"Okay, so maybe we should have checked the temperature first. But still, it's so pretty." She was right, it was pretty. The street was quieter now, and we weren't the only ones strolling down the sidewalk. Monty and I moseyed along, glancing in shop windows and restaurants. I made mental notes of places we could go throughout the week.

"You ready to go back?" I asked. We'd taken so many turns that I wasn't exactly sure how to get back to the hotel, but that's what GPS was for.

"Sure," she said, and then yawned.

Our walk back was even slower.

"We shouldn't have walked so far," Monty said, stopping and looking up at the sky.

"I mean, we could always call a car."

"That's a little much, don't you think?" she said, and then, as if it was fate, a guy peddling a bike taxi started coming toward us.

"Hey! We need a ride!" I yelled, and he rang the bell on the bike and stopped.

"Where to?" he asked, and I named our hotel. Monty sat down with a sigh.

"I wish we had these back home."

We started moving and I enjoyed the wind on my face.

"The closest thing we have is someone giving you a ride on their four-wheeler or tractor." That made her laugh, mostly because it was so true. We lived in a weird place.

Both of us were completely beat when we got back to the hotel, so we took turns taking showers and put on pajamas, but covered up with the fluffy robes we found in the closet. There were also slippers.

"I thought this was going to suck, but it's not sucking as much as I thought," Monty said, resting back against the pillows as I flipped through the channels. I was tired, but not quite ready for sleep yet. I needed some wind-down time first.

"Are you telling me that this sucks?" I waved my hand around the gorgeous room. "Did you need a cute boy rubbing your feet or something? I can probably order that." Room service had to have something like that available.

Monty made a face. "Ew, no. I don't want a man touching my feet, thank you."

Agreed. I didn't even let Gus rub my feet much, and he was my fiancé.

"Is there anything else you do want?" I turned on my side and propped my head on my hand. Monty stared at the ceiling.

"I don't know anything anymore, Cin," she said, and I watched a tear roll down her cheek. I reached up and swiped at it with the sleeve of my robe.

"Hey, talk to me," I said.

Monty pressed her lips together and shook her head.

"I don't know."

"Tell me and I'll help you figure it out." She shook her head again and sniffed. I rolled over and grabbed the box of tissues from the nightstand, passing them to her.

"I really just want to go to bed."

"Okay," I said, and she went to the bathroom for a few minutes. I assumed she was brushing her teeth, but I didn't really know. She came out and her face was a little red. I took my turn, and she was quiet as I tossed the robe on a chair, plugged in my phone, and climbed into bed.

Monty quickly braided her hair back and I settled in next to her.

"Goodnight?" I said, because I couldn't figure out what else to say.

"Yeah, goodnight." She leaned over and turned off the lamp on her side and I turned off mine.

The two of us lay in the dark, listening to each other breathe.

"Thank you for coming with me," she whispered.

"You're welcome."

She rolled away from me and went to sleep.

Chapter Eight

MONTY

I barely slept that first night, but I tried. The nap in the middle of the day hadn't been the best idea, and had thrown my internal clock off, but there were other reasons why I couldn't get my mind to settle.

So many thoughts that were shapeless and confusing and strange. I couldn't talk to Tessa about them, because I didn't even have words for them. Just a sick feeling in my stomach that kept me up all night.

At least Tessa had slept, because I'd heard her tiny adorable snore.

I waited until she stirred before I pretended to come awake. I rolled over and almost smiled at her sleep-drenched appearance. Hair everywhere, eyes bleary, cheeks with marks on them from the pillowcase.

"Good morning sunshine," she said, giving me a little smile before stretching her arms over her head.

"Good morning." She rolled out of bed and headed to the bathroom, and I pulled up my agenda on my phone. I'd left yesterday blank because I knew I probably wouldn't be in the best state to schedule anything, and I'd been right.

Today, though, today I had plans.

Tessa skipped back from the bathroom and jumped on the bed, her eyes bright.

"You're awfully chipper," I said. Usually she wasn't a morning person.

"I couldn't stop thinking about what I was going to order for breakfast. Help me decide." She nabbed the room service menu and shoved it in my face. Normally I would have discouraged all the room service orders, but I had a huge budget for food, so we could pretty much do what we wanted. In an ideal world, TJ and I would have been having too much honeymoon sex to worry about food and would have been ordering it around the clock.

Hindsight, you rude bitch.

"Challah French toast sounds incredible, plus some fruit and coffee? I need some fucking caffeine," Tessa said, and I looked away from her hair. It was stuck up all over the place, like the plumes of an exotic bird.

"Sounds good to me," I said, not even remembering what she'd just said a few seconds earlier. Tessa grabbed the phone as I finger-combed my braid out. Today was going to require so much coffee. I hoped they brought enough, or else I'd have to make some with the little pods in the room to get me going.

My best friend didn't seem to need any coffee, she was bright and full of energy and I had to grit my teeth not to yell at her for being so chipper and perky.

"So," she said, at last coming to rest on the bed like a hummingbird finally taking a break, "what's your agenda for today?"

"Let's have breakfast first," I said. I wasn't ready to do anything else yet.

"Oh come on, tell me." Her eyes sparkled, and then she grabbed for my phone.

"Give it back!" I yelled, reaching for the phone as she stood up on the bed, holding it toward the ceiling. There was no way I was getting up and fighting for it.

"Fine, whatever. It's not like I wasn't going to tell you after I'd had some coffee anyway. I also changed my passcode."

"Too bad for you, but I know all your password patterns." She unlocked the phone and waved it in my direction.

"That's why you have two-factor authentication," she said, bouncing slightly and making the bed move in waves.

"Can you stop please?" I asked. If things didn't improve, I was on the fast-track for a migraine.

"Sure," she said, sitting at the edge of the bed and facing me, scrolling through my phone. I didn't have anything on there I didn't want her to see, and it wasn't worth the effort to snatch it back from her.

"Oh, this is more detailed than I thought. Well done."

"I like being organized," I said.

"I know."

A knock at the door interrupted us and the food arrived. Thank goodness. I went for the coffee first and downed a cup before I even touched any of the food.

"Come on," Tessa said, pulling the cart out toward the balcony. I had to help her with the door, and there was barely enough room for two chairs and the cart, but she seemed happy, so who was I to argue?

"See this? This is perfect." Tessa turned her face up to the sun, and it set her hair on fire. If I said that I wasn't jealous of her hair color, it would be a lie. I'd always been horribly envious. Even when we'd been younger and she'd gotten teased for it and I'd had to comfort her and tell her how lovely it was. Like gold and sunsets mixed together.

I pulled my legs up and set my plate on them, taking little

bites here and there. I was hungry, but eating wasn't exactly a priority. Things were still so…

Unsettled. All those thoughts that didn't make sense, but made all the sense. Tessa hummed happily as she devoured her plate in giant bites and then stared out at the world around us as she sipped her coffee, one knee pulled up.

"So, what are the chances of me talking you out of doing everything you had on that list?" she asked, finally turning to look at me.

"Slim to none. You're on my trip, remember? Did you even look at what I had on there? So much of it's for you." I'd added antique stores and weird shops I knew she'd like, and even selected restaurants that had her favorite things. In fact, there was less on that list for me than there was for her. Everything had been easier that way. What I'd planned for me and TJ didn't matter anymore, and it didn't interest me.

"I hope we can at least take an hour or two of unscheduled time for spontaneous things." I wasn't a fan of spontaneous things, and she knew that.

"What kind of spontaneous things?"

She sighed. "That's the point, Ford. You don't know what they're going to be. Don't you have an English degree?" I threw a grape at her.

"Yes, I know what the word spontaneous means. I'm just not a fan." I shuddered.

"But can't spontaneous things be great sometimes?" she said, leaning forward and plucking a strawberry off the plate and biting into it. The juice stained her lips a little.

"Was it fun when we were almost attacked that family of raccoons when we tried to sneak onto the beach to go to that party that one time? Was it fun when we got a flat tire in the middle of fucking nowhere when you said we should 'just drive and see what happens'?"

"First of all," Tessa said, pointing at me with her fork as

she attacked the leftover bites on my plate, "it's not my fault that we took the wrong path, and at least those raccoons weren't rabid. And second, we had fun waiting for the roadside assistance, and we met a very interesting guy when he showed up and told us all about his exotic bird collection and showed us pictures of the swords he made. I rest my case."

She sat back, triumphant.

"We could have gotten rabies!" I yelled.

"But we didn't. That's the point. And we're not in risk of rabies if I take you off the beaten path for an hour. Can I have an hour? Just one. You can time me."

Tessa knew she was going to win. I was stubborn, but she was stubborner, when she wanted to get her way. Most of the time she was so go-with-the-flow, but when she desired something, she dug her heels in unlike anyone I'd ever seen.

"One hour. But I get to do my stuff first, because I've bought tickets and we have a schedule. You get your hour after lunch." Her eyes narrowed slightly.

"Fine. But I get to pick where we eat."

I hadn't made a reservation yet, but I'd been planning on it. I guess I could bump today's restaurant to another day. That would require some other shuffling, but I could make it happen.

"Deal?" she asked, holding her hand out.

"Deal," I said, and we shook on it.

"NO LOOKING IT UP, we're eating here," Tessa said, dragging me through the doors of the restaurant. It was an odd shade of pink on the outside and looked more like an odd private home than a restaurant, but it looked like it was southern food, so that was promising. I'd have to fight myself not to get fried chicken again. It was quickly becoming my favorite thing and I was determined to crack the perfect recipe when I got home.

Now that I wasn't getting married, I had to find more ways to fill the time I used to spend with TJ.

The pace was pretty on the inside, with tons of paintings and white tablecloths on every table and chandeliers dripping from the ceiling. Swanky. I'd expected Tessa to pick a more casual place. I was glad I'd worn my light and gauzy dress with strawberries on it today. Tessa had surprised me with a pair of black linen pants and a white eyelet t-shirt. I'd been meaning to ask her about it but kept forgetting.

A server seated us at a table near a window and Tessa couldn't stop watching the people walking by.

We got menus and I was relieved to see the place wasn't as expensive as I'd been expecting in my head. Good choice, Tessa. Maybe spontaneity wasn't so bad.

"What are you planning for later?" I asked as we both scanned our menus.

"I'm not planning anything. I mean, I might have looked a few things up to get ideas, but then I decided that wasn't spontaneous, so I'll figure it out after we eat."

So, that was stressing me out a little, but I was still on a little bit of a high from our tour at the Juliette Gordon Low—the founder of the Girl Scouts—historic home, as well as a visit to the Telfair Museum. My brain was overloaded with information and, honestly, it was nice to sit and rest. Every single corner of Savannah had something historical happening in it. It was overwhelming. I also didn't want to forget the darker parts of the city's history, so we'd be diving into that as well.

"I can't decide if I want fish tacos or to go for it and try the gumbo," Tessa said. "What about you?"

"I just really want the fried chicken, but I had fried chicken last night," I said. It even came with a side of mac and cheese, the ideal combination.

"So? Are you only allowed to eat fried chicken once in a twenty-four-hour period?"

"No," I said. "Obviously."

"Then get it."

We both ordered sweet tea, because what else were you going to drink? Tessa decided on the shrimp tacos and I went for the fried chicken.

"See? We might not have come here if you had planned this. So there."

She was right. When I'd been doing my planning, I'd avoided a lot of the more well-known places, and this would have been knocked off my list.

Tessa was cute when she was smug.

We finished lunch, and then I had to just follow her.

"Where are we going?" I asked.

"I don't know," she said, turning around and walking backwards and smiling at me. "That's the point!"

I still wasn't so sure about this.

TESSA SOMEHOW, through her powers of spontaneity, led us to an absolutely gorgeous park with a fountain at the center. It looked like the set of a movie. We even saw more than a few couples in wedding attire taking pictures, and even one wedding progress. The grassy areas were patchworked with blankets and picnickers and children chasing each other all around.

Tessa normally walked fast, as if she was always trying to get to the next thing, but she slowed down and we strolled together.

"See? Isn't this perfect?"

It was.

"Are you ready to admit I was right?" she asked, bumping me with her shoulder.

"Never," I said, shaking my head.

"Come on, admit I was right." She took my arm and made me stop. Our toes touched and she was close enough that I could count the freckles on her cheeks, as if I didn't already know how many she had. I'd been counting those freckles for years. I'd memorized them.

"Never," I whispered.

"What can I do to get you to admit it?" She leaned closer, and my dress fluttered around her legs, wrapping them up.

"Nothing," I said. "There's nothing you can do." I was having trouble swallowing.

"Oh, there's something and I'm going to figure it out. Just you wait." Tessa stepped away from me, and I realized I'd been leaning into her when I ended up stumbling forward and almost falling.

"Whoa, did that sweet tea go to your head?" Tessa said, catching me and helping me stand up again.

"I'm fine," I said.

I didn't know if I was fine.

THE NEXT FEW days were filled with museums, historical walking tours, exploring the cobblestoned streets along the river, multiple trolley tours, and so many incredible foods and drinks. Being in a new place with new air was such a relief, and after that first night, I started sleeping better. There was something about being in a bed with Tessa that calmed my anxieties and let me rest. Or maybe it was being in Savannah. Either way, I didn't ever want to go home.

Every now and then, Tessa would ambush me with "what does it take to make you say I was right?" and usually I would yell because she'd snuck up on me and then I'd say the same thing I'd said before, "nothing."

She was persistent.

Our second to last night, I finally agreed to be spontaneous again.

"Okay, so this isn't technically spontaneous, or at least our outfits aren't going to be," she said as she whipped something shiny out of her suitcase.

"What is that?" I asked as she held up the emerald velvet jumpsuit.

"Well, it *was* what I was going to wear to your wedding, but now it's what I'm wearing tonight. And this," she did another flourish and pulled out one of my favorite dresses, "is what you are wearing. I packed your petticoat and everything." She pulled that out too.

"When did you get this?" I asked, taking the items from her.

"Like a few days before we left? You should probably pay better attention to what's in your closet, Ford." I crushed the fabric to my chest, petting the bronze taffeta skirt.

"I'm going to have to steam this to get the wrinkles out," I said, holding it up. The dress was technically two pieces, a black high-neck crop top that was nearly backless and a bronze taffeta skirt. It made me feel both bookish and glamorous at the same time, especially with that little bit of my torso that peeked between the top and skirt.

"There's a function for that on the iron," Tessa said, pulling that out of the closet and hauling out the ironing board.

"Who are you right now? Have you ever used an iron in your entire life?" I couldn't even imagine it. Tessa picked up the iron and looked at it as if it was going to bite her. "Give me that."

I took it from her and went to put some water in it.

"Just because I've never used one, doesn't mean I don't know how. I've never used a penis, but I'm pretty sure I know what to do with it."

I almost dropped the iron on my foot.

"What did you say?" I came out of the bathroom and set the iron down.

"What?" she said.

"The penis thing. You and Gus have never…" Tessa and I didn't really talk about sex. With TJ, there just hadn't been much to talk about in that department. We did it, and that was about it. Most of the time it was nice, and that was as good as it got. I could always do better on my own, but wasn't that true for everybody?

"I mean, we've done some stuff, but never, like, other stuff." Her entire face, including her ears, were aflame. "It was just a joke, Ford. Calm down."

I wanted to ask her more, but I honestly didn't want to hear the answers, so I dropped it. How was it that Tessa and I could talk about literally anything else, but we couldn't seem to get past this particular topic? Whatever, I didn't need to think about it.

Instead, I focused on fixing my skirt. Tessa and I took turns changing in the bathroom, like we'd done all week. We hadn't even discussed it, that was just what we'd always done. When she came out in her jumpsuit, I had to sit down on the bed because my legs stopped holding me up.

"Okay, so can you see my nipples?" She looked down at the neckline, which was, in a word, plunging. "I taped myself in so I think I'm good." She turned to the side and then back to the front.

Her clavicles and the space between her breasts were visible. She had freckles there, too. I'd seen her in a bathing suit, but this was…entirely different.

"Wait a second, you were going to wear this to my wedding? Like that?" All I could imagine were wardrobe malfunctions and scandalized relatives.

"Hell yeah. For that I was going to use duct tape. And I had this underthing that I could put on at the last minute. But my boobs really look okay?" She looked down again and I was at a complete loss for words.

"You look amazing, Cin," I said finally. She smiled.

"So do you! Can I get a twirl?" I realized I shouldn't have sat down with the dress, so I hopped up and looked at the back to make sure the taffeta still looked okay. The petticoat I wore under it fluffed the skirt out so it was perfect for twirls.

I stepped out and did a few turns for Tessa as she clapped.

"Gorgeous. Are you almost ready?"

"Just need to do my hair and makeup," I said. She rolled her eyes.

"So it's going to take another hour or so?"

I fluffed out my skirt. "Hey, come on now. It doesn't take me that long."

"I'm timing you," she said.

"Fine, then I'm picking the restaurant," I called as I looked at my hair in the mirror, wondering what the heck to do with it. Up was best, so I did a few quick braids and pulled everything back into a twist. Not bad.

"You've got ten minutes, max," Tessa called.

"Calm the fuck down!" I yelled as I got out my makeup bag and set everything on the counter.

"Nine minutes and fifty-five seconds!"

"I'm going to strangle you in your sleep if you don't stop."

"You can't strangle me on our bestfriendimoon."

I took a deep breath and focused on getting my foundation even.

Chapter Nine

*T*ESSA

It wasn't just my imagination that people were staring at Monty. It made sense, because she was fucking gorgeous, and that outfit was perfect for her. I could never pull off something like that. Monty was the kind of person who could wear a shapeless dress and make it look incredible. On me, it would just look like a sack.

I was pretty happy with my own outfit. I'd found it by chance on a rack in the mall and had known it was the perfect thing to wear for her wedding. Now that wasn't happening, I had to get my use out of it.

Monty selected a moody restaurant with smoky drinks and soft music playing in the background and leather on the chairs.

"After tonight, I'm going to get you to admit I was right," I said as we scanned our menus.

"We'll see about that."

I didn't really have a plan of what we were going to do after this, but I wanted to find somewhere fun. Maybe a club or something. Nothing too intense, just somewhere we might be able to shake it and get a drink and let loose. So much of what we'd done during the day was historical. There were so many facts in my brain now that I almost wished I could pour some of them out because it was just too much information. Maybe dancing it out would help.

I couldn't stop looking at Monty in her outfit. Just an absolute knockout. I hoped no dudes tried to hit on her, because that was literally the last thing she needed.

"What are you thinking about?" Monty asked as I sipped my drink. It was alcoholic and had a bunch of stuff I'd never heard of in it, but it was really good. I'd have to remember what it was so I could try and replicate it at home.

"Nothing that concerns you."

Her eyes narrowed. "You're plotting something. I can tell."

"I never plot. At least not in public."

That made her laugh a little. "You look really great. I hope you know that."

"Thanks," she said, her cheeks getting a little pink. "So do you."

"SO, WHERE TO NOW?" We stood outside the restaurant post dinner and chocolate dessert and I tried to pick a direction.

"This way," I said, pointing to the left.

"You have no idea where we're going, do you?"

"Nope! That's the point. I thought we'd been over this."

Monty looked from right to left, as if at any moment someone was going to jump out and attack her. The streets were filled with other people going to dinner or strolling or shopping. It wasn't even that late, and this was a busy area.

I heard some music and it was a good song, so I decided to follow it. We crossed the street and turned a corner and there it was.

"That's where we're going," I said, pointing.

"Okay," Monty said after a little hesitation. Wow, I'd actually expected more resistance, but cool, okay.

We approached the building, which turned out to be a bar that had a bunch of women in leather vests leaning against motorcycles and smoking outside.

"Are you sure we should go in there?" Monty said, holding my arm.

"Yeah, why not?"

"Because I don't think we belong in there," she said.

"Why not?" Looked fine to me. What was her deal?

"Because I think this might be a lesbian bar," she said, and then I saw two women making out right in front of us.

"So? We're women. Just because we aren't lesbians, doesn't mean we can't go in and have one drink. Come on, one drink."

Monty looked up at the brick building as if it was going to swallow her up and never let her go.

"It'll be fine, you're being extra," I said, pulling her toward the door. We had our IDs checked and went in. Yup, definitely a lesbian bar. There were rainbow flags and memorabilia everywhere.

"Listen, Vanessa and Hollie would be mad if I didn't go to this place and then bring back stories and tell them about it," I said.

Monty snorted. "You're probably right."

"Let's get a drink."

We waded through the crowded and I bopped to the beat of the music. It was so crowded that dancing would only be possible if you were okay with bumping into a whole lot of sweaty strangers.

"What can I get you, sweetheart?" the bartender asked. She had two eyebrow rings and more tattooed skin than not. I lost the ability to speak for a moment.

"Uhhhh," I said, looking at Monty. She shook her head, her eyes wide. What was wrong with us?

"How about I make you something special? You'll like it," the bartender said with a wink, and I felt my face get hot. Or maybe it was just the lack of moving air in the room.

She poured a bunch of things together into two copper cups and pushed the drinks toward me and Monty.

"Want to start a tab?" she asked, taking my credit card.

"Sure?" I said. I'd promised Monty only one drink, but why not? The bartender gave me a smile and I picked up my drink with both hands for some reason.

"To the last night of the bestfriendimoon," I said, holding my cup up. It had a lime wedge on the side that I squeezed into the drink and stirred with the tiny black straw.

"I'm not going to call it that," Monty said, holding her cup.

"Come on, just one last time. For me?" I pretended to pout and Monty's eyes went wide for a second and if it wasn't so damn dark in here, I would have sworn she was blushing.

"To the last night of the bestfriendimoon," she mumbled, and we tapped our cups together. I was wary about drinking something without knowing what was in it, but bottoms up!

"Oh, that's nice," I said. The drink was sweet and smoky at the same time, with a tiny hit of mint and something sharp. Ginger, maybe?

"I think it's a Moscow Mule," Monty said, after taking a few sips. "But with something else. I don't know, but it's good. I'll have to be careful or else I'm going to get white-girl wasted on this."

"Same," I said. We sipped and looked around. I kept thinking that we were going to have someone come up to us and ask for a queer card to be here, but it wasn't happening so far. What was happening was getting constantly jostled by other people wanting drinks.

"Do you want to go find somewhere less crowded?" I yelled to Monty, and she nodded.

Since I didn't want her to get swept into the crowd, I grabbed her hand and towed her behind me as we attempted to move through a whole lot of people who didn't want to let us through. I plowed my way forward anyway, and Monty's fingers kept twitching in my hand.

Somehow, I spotted a table that was at chest height and perfect for two people to set their drinks on. I made my way toward it and set my cup down, claiming this table in the name of bestfriendimoon.

"That's better," I said. We were kind of tucked away, so the music wasn't so loud and there weren't as many people. Monty's eyes kept flitting around the room.

"You okay?" I asked. Maybe this had been a bad idea. "Do you want to go?" Someone pushed past me to join their friends at the next closest table, so I had to scoot closer to Monty, our arms touching. They were both bare due to the outfits. Plus, it was kinda sweaty in here.

"No, I'm fine. Just don't feel like we belong here. I'm scared that we're going to get booted."

"I mean, they're not going to check out queer cards, if there were such a thing. You come to Pride with me every year."

"That's different. I feel like I'm an invader."

She finished the rest of her drink, even though she said she was going to drink it slow. Monty looked down into her cup and then at me.

"Want another?"

I was still working on my first, but I nodded my head. Something was off with her, and I couldn't put my finger on it. I could sort of see what she was saying, but weren't we being good allies by supporting the bar and buying drinks? It wasn't like we were here to make fun of people or be homophobic or transphobic.

While I sipped at my drink, I tried to curl back into a corner so I wasn't taking up any space.

"Hey, you here alone?" a voice said. I looked up to find a person with long dark hair and an eyebrow piercing smiling at me. If I had to guess, I'd say she was a few years older than me and clearly lifted a few weights. Her shoulders were barely contained by her tank. I wanted to congratulate her on all her work, but my mouth was completely dry.

"I'm Lucinda," she said, leaning closer to me. "Can I buy you a drink?"

Oh. OH.

She was hitting on me. The realization hit me like a train and I almost fell over, even though I was leaning on the table. I was getting hit on at a gay bar and I didn't really know what to do in this situation.

Before I could come up with anything to tell this person I was a heterosexual, an arm snaked around me and a soft voice spoke right next to my ear.

"Hey, babe, who's this?"

I almost fell over again, but Monty's arm was tight around me so I didn't go anywhere.

"Oh, sorry," Lucinda said, backing off. "Nice to meet you." And then she was gone, and I was dizzy and wondering if this was real life.

Monty

I couldn't put a name to the feeling that blazed through me when I saw someone talking to Tessa. It was hot and unpleasant and it completely consumed me until I could barely breathe. I walked away from the bar, completely abandoning

94

the drinks, and what I did next made no sense, but I had moved without thinking.

My arm wound around her, pulling her close and I looked right at the other person, telling her with my entire being that she was treading too close to something that did not belong to her. Her eyes went wide and she left, but I would have fought her if she persisted. I would have ripped her to shreds and not have even thought twice about it.

"You're shaking," Tessa said, turning to look at me. I still had my arm clamped around her, and it was an effort to remove it.

"I'm sorry," I said, and suddenly I was so embarrassed that I wanted a portal to open up in the floor and suck me into a different dimension where I would forget what I'd just done.

Unable to do anything else, I picked up Tessa's drink and downed it. Tessa blinked at me. It might be dim in here, but I would have seen her blush flashing like a neon sign in the darkest, deepest cave. She must be totally embarrassed by me.

This little venture had been a huge mistake.

"We should go," I said, looking into the empty cup. I wasn't much of a drinker, so I was on the road to making even more bad decisions.

"Okay," she said.

THE ONLY TALKING we did on the way back was Tessa telling me where to turn so we didn't get lost.

"I'm sorry," I said as we stepped into the hotel lobby. Thunder rumbled in the distance. The forecast was for storms all night.

"For what?" she said, not meeting my eyes.

"For...that," I said. I couldn't even put words to what "that" was. "For being a total weirdo back there."

People kept walking by us, and we moved to the side of the lobby, where a few chairs grouped around a small table. I fell into one of them. Tessa sat next to me.

"It's fine," she said, and I waited for her to say more. Tessa always had more to say. The only time I ever got truly worried about her was when she wasn't talking. "I'm tired, can we go upstairs?"

Her eyes kept darting around, like she didn't want anyone to see her or something.

"Yeah," I said, and we got in the elevator significantly less upbeat than we'd been when we'd left.

TESSA WENT RIGHT for the shower when we got back to the room. I sat by the sliding glass door and watched raindrops patter and slide down the glass and lightning split itself across the sky.

I needed to get out of my skirt, but I couldn't do anything. Something was happening to me and I couldn't even move. The thoughts I'd had off and on and that had stalked my dreams were bubbling up, and I was powerless to stop them.

Something was happening. Something *big*. Something that I'd never be able to go back from.

Tessa came out of the bathroom in her pajamas, her hair wet and falling on her forehead. I wanted to push it back and out of her eyes.

"You want to go?" she asked, rubbing a towel on her hair. I wanted to tell her not to do that, it was going to make her ends split, but I couldn't. There was too much else going on inside me that she wasn't even aware of.

"Yeah," I said, somehow getting to my feet. They moved without me noticing and the next thing I knew, I was turning off the shower and getting out. I'd forgotten to bring clothes in with me, but Tessa must have put them on the counter for me while I'd been under the water.

My hair dripped down my back, making a little puddle on the floor.

I wasn't the same person I'd been when I'd gotten into the shower and I desperately needed to talk to someone about it.

The only one I had was Tessa.

Chapter Ten

TESSA

Monty was acting totally strange ever since we'd walked into that bar, and I didn't know how to ask her what was going on. She came out of the shower and found me sitting in front of the sliding glass doors with the lights off, watching the lightning.

"Remember when we used to do this?" I asked her.

"And your mom would make frappes," she said, coming to sit beside me.

"Let's order some from room service," I said, hopping up. I called the order in and grabbed the wide-tooth comb that she used to detangle her hair.

"Come on, you didn't even brush it out. Are you okay?" She turned and presented me her back. I dabbed at her hair with the towel before dividing it into sections and, starting at the ends, began gently pulling the comb through.

"I have something to tell you," she whispered. Lightning lit up the room, and I was interrupted from answering her by the arrival of the frappes. I tipped the server and handed her a frosted glass. She took it in both hands.

"What is it, Ford?" I asked. My hands shook as I kept working on her hair.

She moved away from me and scooted around so we were face-to-face. I picked up my frappe and gulped so much that I almost choked.

Monty set hers down next to her and then lay down on the floor, looking at the ceiling. I joined her, our shoulders touching. I'd just have to keep track of where I'd put my frappe glass. Cleaning that shit off the carpet would be a nightmare.

Thunder boomed so close that I jumped a little.

"Even if I didn't know you better than I know myself, I'd know something was going on with you. Something big. Can you find somewhere to start?" I asked.

Monty took a deep breath and licked her lips.

"When I found out about TJ cheating, I was angry. But I was also relieved. I didn't want to marry him. I don't think I ever did. I just…I made a plan that I was going to be librarian and marry a man and I never questioned it. He was there and he asked. It was what I was supposed to do. Everyone said so. Girls would tell me all the time how lucky I was and how hot he was, and I repeated all of that over and over to myself in the dark at night. I was lucky. So lucky. But that didn't make it true."

I clamped my lips shut so I didn't make any comment. I had to shut up so she could get this out. She needed to get it all out. My arms ached to hold her, but I pressed them against my sides.

"I had everything planned, Tessa. Everything. There was so much comfort in knowing exactly where I was going. Exactly what my path was. I didn't have to rattle around or worry or have a crisis about who I was going to be. I already knew. I knew, Tessa. I knew who I was."

She took a deep breath.

"Until now."

This waiting was going to kill me. I felt like I was standing on the edge of a cliff with her, waiting to see what would happen.

"I've been thinking, and I think I know…I don't think I'm…" she trailed off and made a gasping noise that was almost like a sob. I couldn't stay still anymore, so I rolled over and faced her. I still didn't speak, but I couldn't look away from her face. She kept her eyes on the ceiling as she inhaled and exhaled with little jerks. I looked for tears, but there were none that I could see. There was nothing I could do to help her, and it was one of the worst feelings in the world.

"I don't think I attracted to men. At all. I'm not sure. I was having all these thoughts and now that my future is this big blank and I'd started letting myself imagine what it *could* be, not what it *should* be, and I don't think I want it to be with a guy. Not just because of TJ. Looking back now, it feels obvious that I was never really attracted to him. I mean, sure, he was good looking. I knew that on the surface. But when he kissed me, I felt nothing. Just two sets of lips touching. When we first got together I'd get so nervous when he'd kiss me, but once that went away it was like kissing a relative. No fire. No desire. No feeling like I wanted him to do it again."

For some reason, I started shaking. Maybe I was cold from the frappe. I almost screamed as another boom of thunder sounded right above us, so loud that it almost shook the hotel. Rain smashed against the windows, as if it was trying to find a way in.

"And I know that someone else might say that just means I wasn't attracted to TJ, but that's not it. I can't explain it. I don't understand it. I just know that it's true. It's true that I'm some form of gay or queer or something. I don't know."

She exhaled slowly and I waited for her to say more.

"Please say something," she whispered.

"How long have you been thinking about this?" The questions piled up in my mind, but I needed them to shut up right now. Supporting Monty was the absolute most important thing I could do right now.

"I don't know, exactly. Off and on since the breakup. But this trip really opened something up in me, and being at that bar tonight." She shivered. "It was like sticking a key into a lock and opening a box in my brain that I didn't know was there."

I'd had a lot of experience with queer people. Hell, I had two trans lesbian aunts. But nearly everyone had been out before I'd known them. This was a new experience, and this was my best friend.

I had to find the right words. I desperately wished I could talk with my aunts, because they'd know exactly what to say.

"I love you, always. You're my best friend and I'll do whatever you need to help you work through this, and you have my support. And I love you. Did I say that already?"

Sweat collected on my upper lip and the air in the room felt thick for a moment.

"Thanks, that means a lot. It's kind of mind-blowing that you can not know yourself so thoroughly. You know?"

Not really, but I nodded anyway.

"Do you want a hug?" I asked her.

"Yeah," she said. Her arms came around me and we lay on the floor together, our noses just inches apart. It was impossible to tell which sound was louder: the thunder or the beating of my heart.

"Thank you for telling me. I know that wasn't easy."

"Thank you for being my best friend. I knew you were the first person I needed to talk to about it with. I'm so messed up, Tess."

Now the tears started and I used my thumbs to wipe them away.

"You're not messed up. You're just figuring yourself out. Some people don't even do that their entire lives."

She sniffed and I wished I had a tissue handy. "But how could I not know? Is my entire fucking life a lie? Am I a lesbian? Am I bi? What am I even supposed to do now?"

The words tumbled out of her mouth in a rush, all tangling together, her eyes wide with panic.

I held her face in my hands and met her eyes.

"We'll figure it out. You don't have to do anything right now. You're safe with me, and if you want to talk about it or don't want to talk about it, let me know. Okay?"

"Okay," she whispered.

"I'm going to get you some tissues." Reluctantly, I let go of her and scooted over to the nightstand and pulled down the box of tissues.

"I can't believe this is happening," she said, after she'd wiped her nose and her face. "Do I have to start wearing flannel and buy a bunch of power tools? I don't even know what to do with this."

"I don't think there's one way to be queer, but if you want to know about either of those things, my aunts are only a phone call away. They'd be happy to take you under their wing and teach you their ways."

She snorted and I breathed a sigh of relief. I didn't want this to be an upsetting moment for her. I wanted her to know how much I loved her and wanted her to be happy.

"So, can I finally say how much I fucking hated TJ?" I asked.

Monty narrowed her eyes and glared at me. "That was never in question, Cin. I knew you hated him. You are not as subtle as you think you are."

"That's a lie, I can be very subtle." I picked up my frappe and almost dropped the glass.

"It's fine, I didn't like him either. What was I thinking?"

A flash of lightning lit up the room.

"Hey, we all make bad decisions. Remember when I thought I'd look great with bangs and cut them myself while attempting to follow a video?"

Monty picked up her frappe and sat up, pulling her knees close.

"I told you that was a bad idea, but you didn't listen."

I sputtered into my glass, almost spraying frappe everywhere. "You were the one who handed me the scissors!"

"Because you were going to use kid's scissors and would have made it even worse! I gave you the right pair of scissors and the rest was up to you. I was not responsible for anything you did after."

"You are so full of shit right now and I should dump this on your head, but I won't. You're welcome." I held up my frappe and leaned toward her.

Monty pointed at me with one finger. "Don't you even dare, Tessa O'Connell."

I stuck the straw back in my mouth and sipped. "I wouldn't want to waste this."

"Just don't mess with me or you'll wake up with bad bangs again."

NO IDEA HOW MONTY SLEPT, but I couldn't stop thinking about everything she'd told me. Should I have known? I mean, that was ridiculous because *she* didn't even know. Sure, I'd hated TJ, but I probably would have hated just about any guy because he wasn't good enough for her. I'd sucked it up and kept my mouth shut as much as I could because she asked me to.

Now that he was out of the picture, she could be free and figure out what she wanted, and I was going to be by her side for every single step. Coming out was a huge deal, and I didn't want her to feel forced or like she owed anyone anything. Her parents weren't all that supportive in anything she did, so there was probably going to be no support there, but she'd all but severed ties with them years ago. My parents, of course, would have completely open arms, so no stress there.

This had been quite the trip for both of us, and tomorrow we had to get on a plane and go back to our regular lives, both holding her secret and keeping it safe.

To pass the time until she woke up, I made a mental list of all the books she could read. If there was one thing I could do, it was recommend a book. Sure, she was a librarian, and probably knew about most of the titles I came up with already, but I wanted to contribute in some way.

The other thing I couldn't stop going over was her behavior in the lesbian bar. It was probably just dealing with her sexuality, but that didn't explain why she'd acted so possessive when Lucinda (what a gorgeous name) had tried to hit on me, which I wasn't even sure that's what she'd been doing. I was probably just making too much of it. She was probably just trying to be nice to someone who looked like she was in from out of town. She'd had a soft southern accent that I envied.

I mean, I was as straight as could be, I just knew a lot of queer people. And now one more, I guess.

MONTY WAS WITHDRAWN, but contemplative, on the trip back home. I honestly wasn't looking forward to having to go back to my life, but I'd missed my family and Gus and the bookstore, so it was a mixed bag.

"Call me later, okay?" I asked, as she dropped me off at home after a seriously delayed flight. I wanted to ask her to come in, but I also knew she needed some time alone to decompress after being on the plane and being in a new place. I also really needed a shower and a nap. Knowing Monty, the first thing she'd do when she got home would be unpack her suitcase and do a load of laundry. Overachiever.

"I will. And thank you. For coming with me and for everything else."

I pulled her in for a tight hug and smacked a kiss on her cheek.

"I'm always here if you need me, Ford, even though bestfriendimoon is over and you never admitted I'm right."

Although I couldn't see her face, I could feel her rolling her eyes.

"I love you too, and I'll never admit it."

COMING BACK to reality was rough. Even though I'd been in the same time zone, I was still convinced I had jetlag, even though Monty insisted that was impossible.

"Listen, time moves differently on planes," I said a few days later, when we were walking on the beach in the surf.

"Have you unpacked your suitcase yet?" she asked, leaning down to pick up a shell before discarding it. Monty always ended up with pockets full of shells and interesting rocks when we came here. She had an incredible knack for finding seaglass, which was so rare now with the profusion of plastic bottles.

"No comment," I said. We both knew I hadn't.

"What am I going to do with you?" She smiled and shook her head.

A seagull waddled along ahead of us as three children threw themselves into the waves with screams.

"Have you thought anymore about what we talked about in Savannah?" She hadn't brought it up and I'd been giving her space the past few days.

"It's been pretty much all I've thought about, honestly. I've been a mess at work because I can't think of anything else. The reading list has been helpful for when I can't sleep." It hadn't escaped my notice that she'd also seemed exhausted since we got back.

We took a few more steps and I could feel she was working up to something.

"So, I think I'm a lesbian. I guess. Or something like that. It's so complicated, and I'm afraid I'm going to lock myself into a label and then if I want to change later I'll feel trapped. It's all so much to consider. I know I'm definitely not ready to tell anyone else yet."

She picked up a small stone, rubbing it free of sand before deciding it was a keeper and sliding it into her shorts pocket.

"So yeah. I'm sort of a lesbian. I think."

"You can always just use queer if you want." Not that I was the authority, being cis, alloromantic, and heterosexual.

"Yeah, that might be best for now. Until I can figure out if something fits better. It's a little different than trying on a sweater." She laughed softly.

"Yeah, I'm guessing it is." I didn't know what she was going through, but I could sympathize, completely.

"And I think once I get a better handle on things, I might like to talk to your aunts. I mean, they feel like my aunts too, since I'm not close with my own family. You kind of absorbed me into yours."

"It's true. You assimilated into the O'Connell clan. Your copy of the manual and poster of the family crest is in the mail." We both laughed about that and the wind whipped her hair in front of her face and I helped her push it back.

"Please don't tell Gus, okay?" she said.

"Of course. He's my second-best friend, but you'll always be my first. Just don't tell him that."

Her hair was almost reddish in the light of the sunset.

"I think he already knows he's second."

"I'm totally putting that in our vows," I said.

We resumed walking.

"Have you picked a date yet?"

I made a face. "I'm still hoping that I can pull off an elopement."

Monty just gave me a look.

"I still need to give you your wedding present. I kind of hid it away with the rest of your shit, but do you think you'd be okay if I gave it to you now? I don't want you to associate it with the breakup and everything. Shit, can you think of if you'd actually married him?"

Monty closed her eyes. "I think about that all the time. I've honestly almost texted TJ and thanked him for cheating on me, as much as it hurt. Because it set me free." She opened her eyes and tipped her head up, smiling at the clouds.

"I'm happy for you," I said. "I really am. Plus, no more TJ!" That was something to celebrate in and of itself.

"No more TJ," she said through a sigh. "Maybe there's room for someone new. Who knows?"

I stopped walking. "Wait, are you ready to date?" That seemed awfully fast.

"No, no definitely not. Just pondering the possibilities." She twirled in a circle and started walking backwards.

I didn't want to think about her dating again. It was bad enough when she'd been with TJ and I'd had to hang out with him. What if she found another person I didn't like?

"They better get my stamp of approval. I didn't get to approve TJ and look how that turned out."

She shrugged and did a little skip. She seemed lighter than she had a few moments ago, and I was glad to see it, but also wary.

"We'll see," she said, and then she started running, laughing as her feet kicked up water.

"What are you doing?" I started jogging to keep up with her. A memory flashed of the two of us in half-dry bathing suits, chasing each other down this very beach years before.

I'd lived my whole life beside Monty. There was no life before her that I could remember. She'd always been there, and now things were changing for her. Sure, when she'd been engaged to TJ, I'd known that she was going to get married and that would change things, but my efforts to put that out of my mind as much as I could had been pretty effective. Now that wasn't happening and I had her all to myself again. But for how long?

"Wait for me!"

Chapter Eleven

MONTY

I was queer now. Possibly a lesbian. I'd done a lot of looking online to figure it out, and my current hobby was trying to decide which celebrities I found the hottest.

So much was so obvious now. I'd never had one ounce of desire for TJ. When I had sex with him, it wasn't like being on my own. Sure, it felt nice, but that was about it. I'd faked every single orgasm, mostly because I just didn't care. That was the other thing I should have known: I didn't *care* about him. When I wasn't with him, I sometimes forgot he even existed. Before I'd had a ring on my finger, I had to set reminders to call or text him.

He hadn't been that into me, either, which made the fact that he'd proposed so strange. I'd probably never know what was truly going through his mind when he'd asked me to marry him, or why he'd stayed with me so long. I was one to talk; I'd been ready to marry a man I didn't even love.

There were almost too many online resources about being queer, and too many discussions that I didn't feel like I was a part of, so I stuck with reading fiction (mostly romances) and looking through pictures of beautiful women.

Not a bad way to spend my time, to be honest. I was really getting into it. Did I have a type? Did I have a preference? I had no idea. It was a bit like being a preteen picking which member of a band was the hottest. Only I guess I'd usually picked the one with the best hair. Huh.

There was so much to think about, and more often than not, I started feeling like I was getting a headache and had to stop, or switch to reading romances or watching lots of TV shows. Somehow, I had cut myself off from so much content, probably because I was afraid it would trigger something in me.

Everything made sense from this hindsight point.

Now that I had a better handle on myself, I had some decisions to make. I didn't care about telling my parents, but there were a few key people I did want to trust, the top one being Tessa. She already knew, so I didn't have to go through that again. Next on my list: Tessa's parents, Gus, and Tessa's aunts. I wanted to tackle the aunts first, so after locking up the library one day the following Thursday, I headed over to the antique store, knowing they stayed open later on Thursdays. I hadn't told Tessa I was doing this, because I wanted to just do it.

"Oh, Monty, good to see you!" Vanessa came out from behind the register to give me a warm hug. "Is Tessa with you?"

I shook my head. "Actually, I came to see you. And Hollie, if she's around. If not, can we talk?"

"Of course, sweetheart."

As if she'd heard her name, Hollie came around the corner.

"Monty, what are you doing here?"

"Do you want to go somewhere more quiet?" Vanessa asked.

"Yeah, sure."

Why had I decided to do this? Coming out to Tessa was one thing, but this was completely different. Was it different every time?

Vanessa and Hollie took me back to their cozy office, which had two antique desks, and a corner with two chairs and a coffee cart.

"Do you need anything?"

"A glass of water," I croaked, my throat parched.

"Honey, what's wrong?" Hollie said, reaching out and taking one of my hands as Vanessa handed me a glass. I downed the whole thing and set the glass down so I wouldn't drop it.

"I think I'm queer. I mean, I know I am. Maybe a lesbian. I'm still working on that part. But I know you're both lesbians, so I wanted to talk to you about it." I looked into my lap as I spoke.

Hollie squeezed my hand. "I'm so proud of you."

Then I was engulfed in the most loving aunt hug of my life.

"How do you feel?" Vanessa said, pulling back and beaming at me.

"I'm not really sure? But good, I think. There's just so much going on in my head and I'm realizing that I didn't know myself as well as I thought I did." They exchanged a knowing look.

"Thank you so much for trusting us with this," Vanessa said. "I know we don't talk about how we each came out, but if you want to know my story, I'm happy to share it with you."

"Me too," Hollie said.

So I sat with my adopted trans lesbian aunts and listened. Yes, their stories were complicated further by coming to the realization they were transgender first, and transitioning, and then meeting and falling in love with each other.

Still, their stories hit a deep place inside me, and by the

time they'd pushed a cup of steaming minty tea into my hands, I felt lighter.

"You've always been ours, you know," Vanessa said. "Something we both know is that family is what you make of it. The bonds you choose can be thicker than blood."

Hollie's family hadn't been supportive of her, but Vanessa's (Tessa's family) had been, so in a way she'd been adopted by them, kind of like they'd done with me.

"Thank you," I said, finishing my tea. It was late and I needed to go home and figure out what I wanted to make for dinner, and if I was ready to tell Tessa's parents and Gus.

I was engulfed in another aunt hug and they walked me to the front door of the now-dark shop.

"Now, I know we're too old to give you much advice, but there are a lot of queer people your age on social media. If you ever decide you want to try role-playing games, we can hook you up with some friends of friends," Vanessa said.

"She doesn't want to hang out with a bunch of nerds," Hollie said.

"Hey!" Vanessa and I said at the same time.

I COULDN'T STOP SMILING that night. So far, so good on coming out. I knew that it wasn't going to be all roses and rainbow flags, but this was a good sign.

"I'm a lesbian," tried saying as I dipped chicken strips in flour, buttermilk, and then breadcrumbs to fry up for dinner.

"I'm a lesbian," I said as I washed my hair in the shower.

"I'm a lesbian," I said as I brushed my teeth in the mirror, spitting toothpaste everywhere.

The word felt foreign on my tongue, but I liked the sound of it. I liked the weight of it, sitting on my shoulders like and invisible shawl.

"I'm a lesbian," I whispered into the dark as I lay in bed.

"I'm a lesbian," I said to Tessa five minutes later when I called her.

"Well hello to you too. So, you settled on that label?" She sounded tired, but I was too wired and I needed to talk to my best friend.

"Yeah. It feels right, at least right now. So yes. I am a lesbian. I talked to your aunts tonight. They told me how they came out and transitioning and everything."

Tessa yawned. "Sorry. Yeah, They're pretty amazing. Were they helpful?"

"Yeah, they were."

"Did they give you lessons on how to be a lesbian?"

"Uh, no? What kind of lessons would those be?"

"Oh, you know, how to wear a beanie and fix a sink and shit," she said.

"Tessa, those are just stereotypes. There's no one right way to be a lesbian."

"That sounds like something a lesbian would say."

"Oh my god, I'm sorry I called you."

She laughed in my ear. "Sorry, I couldn't help myself. Do you need help sleeping?"

I hadn't realized that I did need to hear her voice tell me silly things as I drifted off.

"Maybe just for a few minutes."

"Ford, you know when I get started that I don't know how to stop. Anyway, since we haven't done this in a while, I've got stuff saved up."

Of course she did. When we'd been on our trip, if we'd stayed up a little late, she'd talked to me like she used to over the phone, but somehow it was different, having her right there. I was too busy being aware of her to listen to what she'd been saying.

"I read the book that inadvertently started the Satanic

Panic from the 80s and 90s. You wanna hear about it?" Her voice perked up and I felt my body sink into my mattress.

"Yeah, I want to hear about it."

IT TOOK me another week to come out to Gus and Tessa's parents. The whole process was exhausting, and I didn't know how I was going to keep doing this. Fortunately, I didn't have to field too many questions from everyone I'd told so far, but I knew that trend wasn't going to continue.

"I'm going to give this to you. It's a 'congrats on being a lesbian' present now," Tessa said, presenting me with a box the following weekend.

Her parents were out, so we had her house to ourselves.

"Okay," I said, taking the box with suspicion. I wasn't sure about this.

"Come on, it's good. My aunts helped me pick it out." That was promising, and Tessa usually gave extremely thoughtful gifts.

The wrapping job was kind of a mess, proof Tessa had done it herself, but that made it all the more special.

"Oh, Tessa, this is beautiful." Inside I'd revealed a small sterling silver tea set, complete with cups, a tray, plates, spoons, and little containers for cream and sugar.

"They didn't have the teapot, so sorry about that."

"It's perfect," I said, wiping away a few tears. It was.

"Come on, let's break it in!" Tessa jumped up and went to heat some water.

"But it's so pretty," I said. "I don't want to hurt it."

"It was made to be used, silly. Also, there's a polishing and cleaning kit in the bottom of the box. A new hobby for you."

She'd thought of everything.

"I love it so much, thank you." I hugged her and held her close. She beamed at me.

"I'm so happy you like it."

The kettle whistled and Tessa went to shut it off.

"What kind of tea would you like, milady?" She held out the box of tea bags to me and I selected an Earl Grey. Seemed appropriate.

"This feels so decadent." We sat on the living room couch sipping from the silver cups.

"I feel so fancy," Tessa said. "Remember that time when I tried to throw that tea party?"

I made a face. "Don't remind me. I can't drink red wine now because of that."

"Hey, it's not my fault that the bottle wasn't labeled. I thought it was juice or something." Tessa had decided to throw me a tea party one summer when we were younger and had grabbed a bottle of homemade wine from her aunts to mix with iced tea to pour in the cups. I'd drunk a bunch of it and ended up puking in the hedges in front of the house. Much drama had ensued.

"I was trying to be classy, and I failed," she said with a sigh.

"It's okay, I still love you."

Her phone made noise and she read a new message.

"Hey, what about telling my brothers? Are you up for that? Keep in mind that if you tell them, they will make shirts to support you."

Oh god, they would. I didn't think I was ready for that quite yet.

"No, let's hold off."

"Fair enough."

We rinsed out the cups and dried them carefully before I packed them back into the box to take back to my apartment.

"Hey, so you wanna watch this new show? I was looking for

stuff to watch and I think there are lesbians in it," Tessa said, turning on the TV.

"I don't have to watch something just because there are lesbians in it."

"I know, but don't you want to?"

"I mean, yes."

She grinned at me. "Exactly."

Tessa put the show on and scooted close to me. "Can you play with my hair?"

When we'd been younger and I'd been practicing my braiding skills, Tessa used to let me work on her hair. Now that it was much shorter, that was harder, but I could still mess with it a little bit.

"Sure," I said. She lay her head in my lap and I dragged my fingers through her curls. It was soothing for me as well.

Aside from polishing the tea set, which wouldn't take too long, I needed a new hobby. Maybe I could take a class or learn a language.

The show was cute and bright and so far, it seemed pretty gay, not that I was much of a judge. I was hooked by the fourth episode, and if she didn't say anything, I was going to go home and marathon this thing.

"Can you pick out a wedding dress for me?" Tessa asked. I'd honestly thought she'd fallen asleep.

"What?"

She sat up. "Can you pick out a wedding dress for me? I know I need to get one like, a year in advance, and I have no idea what I want. You pick one out for me. You'll know what looks good."

I paused the show. "Have you tried any on?"

"No."

"I think you should do that before you give me complete control over what you wear. That's an important day, and you want to wear something you like."

116

My own wedding dress was in storage at my parent's house. I still loved it and wish it wasn't tied to such awful memories. Too bad I couldn't wear it for something else, but it was very clearly a wedding dress.

"Can I just use yours?" she asked.

"Uh, no. I don't think it would fit you, anyway." My dress was a ballgown with lots of tulle and lace and 3/4 lace sleeves. Not Tessa style at all.

"It was worth a shot. Will you go with me? If I go try them on."

She looked up at me, her eyes wide and pleading.

"Listen, if we go and try them on, your mom is going to kill us for not inviting her. And your aunts would want to be there too."

"But if we just go to look and not try on? Just to see what I might like. It would be a shame if I did an appointment and wasted a bunch of time trying on dresses and never picked one. So this is more of a research trip."

That did make sense.

"Okay."

Tessa jumped off the couch. "Okay, let's go."

"Wait, now?"

"Why not? Come on." She pulled me up from the couch. I should be used to Tessa's spontaneous plans, but I wasn't.

"Don't we have to have an appointment?" I protested, as she dragged me through the door and out to her car.

"Not to look. I just want to see. It'll be fun!"

Over an hour later, Tessa was parking her car in the lot at the closest mall and I was staring up at a chain bridal store.

"Come on, you know it'll be a good time." She nudged me. Not that long ago she'd been so down on getting a dress and now she seemed totally pumped, so I had no idea what was going on.

"You owe me dinner," I said.

"Deal."

We walked into the store and were greeted by a smiling consultant asking if we had an appointment.

"We're just here to look, if that's okay? But I do want to make an appointment," Tessa said.

"That's fine, just let me know if you need anything!" The consultant dashed off to help a group that was looking at bridesmaid dresses.

"You know, we could have looked at stuff online," I said. The racks and racks of dresses on the right side of the store were completely overwhelming. Where did you even start?

I'd picked my dress out online and then tried it on at a tiny boutique a few hours away from home and it had been perfect.

"Come on," Tessa said, threading her arm through mine. "Just go with it."

"I hate it when you say that."

"I know," Tessa sang. "What do you think of this one?" She yanked out the first dress on the front of the rack. This was going to be a long afternoon.

Chapter Twelve

TESSA

Honestly, I wasn't excited about trying dresses on, but looking through them was fun as hell. I liked finding a dress that I would rather drop dead than wear, and that turned out to be a lot of them.

"I think I want more simple," I said. "Like, no glitter or sequins or lace. That stuff makes my skin itchy."

"What about this?" Monty said, pulling out a dress that was long and white and sleek. It almost looked like more of an evening gown than a wedding dress.

"Look at the back," she said, turning it around. The back dipped low and had a few strands of what looked like crystals crossing the gap.

"See, that's more like it. Okay, hold on." I took a picture of the dress and the tag so I would know for later when I came back with my mom and aunts and Monty to do the official try on. I was going to put that shit off as long as possible.

"You might want to get it soon, or else it might go out of season, or might get sold," Monty said. She had a point, but whatever. I didn't want to put on a wedding dress yet. We still hadn't decided anything else, not even a date, so why did I need a dress?

"You could always go casual and wear pants." The store did have a few unconventional wedding looks.

"If only my jumpsuit was white, I could walk down the aisle in that." If only. Then I wouldn't have to try anything on.

"I think that would scandalize a lot of your guests."

"Good. People should be regularly scandalized. It's good for them. Builds character."

She laughed.

Somehow we made it through all the racks and my eyes were starting to burn from staring at so much white.

"Come on, I'm hungry," I said.

"Thank god." She sagged against the rack. "I'm starving."

We left the shop and ended up going to a semi-fancy chain restaurant with a massive menu and enormous desserts.

"See, wasn't this worth the trip?" I said as we stuck our forks into a piece of cheesecake that was the size of a small child.

"For this, yes."

"Wait, was being around the dresses hard for you? Shit, I didn't think about that, I'm sorry."

She shook her head and waved her fork in the air as she spoke. "No, it's not that. I don't think, anyway. It's just not knowing what my future is going to look like has been really stressful lately. This helps."

We'd agreed to get a salted caramel cheesecake and it was orgasmic. I was definitely going to make Gus take me here sometime.

I really needed to get more used to the idea that we were getting married. That I'd be moving in with him to his little cabin near the pond. He'd inherited it from his grandparents and it was idyllic. We'd probably get a few dogs and go paddleboarding on the weekends. In the evenings I'd read and he'd fiddle around in the shed with woodworking projects.

Still, our wedding was at least a year away. Did I have to let it consume my every waking moment? No, I don't think so.

"You are awfully contemplative over there, Cin."

While I'd been navel-gazing, she'd been attacking the cheesecake and now there wasn't a whole lot left for me. I had to get my act together or else she was going to finish it before I got to have another bite.

"Just thinking about life." That wasn't a lie.

"What about it?"

I didn't want to talk to Monty about this shit.

"That I need more cheesecake in my life. Definitely. We should get some to go." Monty got so excited about the prospect of cheesecake that she didn't pry further about what I'd been thinking about.

My parents were home when we returned, and I was patting myself on the back for deciding to get another piece of cheesecake for them. I never would have heard the end of it if I hadn't brought some home for everyone. What I didn't count on was my brother Mike and his wife Bekah coming over to have dinner with my parents, so I didn't win with everyone.

"How the hell was I supposed to know you were coming over?" I yelled.

"I told you a week ago that we were coming over!" he yelled back.

"Children, please," Mom said halfheartedly. With four of us the house had been loud. The neighbors had complained so many times we'd lost count. It wasn't my fault that the boys were loud. I was also the youngest, so if they were loud, I had to be louder.

"Whatever, Mike. It's not like you know anything about my life." This was a total dig, because I was actually extremely close with my brothers. I saw all of them at least once a week, if not more. I'd seen Donny earlier today, and Ben was dropping by the bookstore tomorrow to get some books because his wife, Annabelle, was pregnant with their first child and he was a nervous wreck. Now I had two sisters-in-law pregnant at the same time and it was going to be a chaotic Christmas at the O'Connell house. I was over the moon about getting new niblings. I adored my niece, Cadence, and couldn't wait for her to get a sibling.

"Will you two just hug and stop being ridiculous?" Bekah said. She'd been ignoring us this whole time. She and Mike had been together since high school, so she'd had enough of our shit. Tessa had been on her phone the entire time and hadn't even been paying attention to our nonsense.

Mike and I smiled at each other and he picked me up in a big hug.

"I love you, Firework." He kissed the top of my head and set me down.

"Yeah, yeah," I said. "Love you too."

Monty left a few minutes later. I really wanted to ask her to stay, but there was no reason now. She was all-in on her new lesbian life and had other shit to do, I guess.

"Thank you again for the tea set. I love it so much."

"You're welcome, Ford."

She waved goodbye with her free hand as she walked to her car with the tea set box.

"What's up with Monty? She seemed quiet," Mike said.

"Well, she did just find out that her fiancé was cheating on her, maybe it has something to do with that?" I said, and his face went red.

"Shit, I forgot about that, sorry."

I shared a look with my mom. Yes, my parents knew, but they'd been sworn to secrecy, and I knew they would keep their word to Monty. She wasn't ready for anyone outside of her inner circle yet, and that was fine.

"Babe, it's late and I have to work early." Bekah was a nurse and sometimes worked weird shifts at the hospital, so she was exhausted most of the time.

Once they'd left, I sat down on the couch with Mom.

"What did you kids get up to today?"

I didn't want to talk about the wedding dress trip. Because then my mom would get all excited and she'd pull out the bridal magazines that she'd been hoarding for years and I would never hear the end of it.

"I gave her the tea set and she loved it and we went on a little road trip to the mall." There, that was completely truthful.

"Isn't there a huge bridal shop in that mall? We should call and make an appointment, you know." Shit, the topic had found me anyway.

"Yeah, sure," I said.

"You have to order your dress at least a year in advance. You can't put this off, Tessa." I was suddenly so very tired.

"Uh huh," I said, getting up. "I'm going to bed."

I lay in bed messing around on my phone before I video called Tessa.

"Didn't we just spend all day together?" she said, smiling softly at me. She was in her room and the lights were off.

"Don't we spend most days together? I mean, we used to spend all day at school with each other and then we'd have sleepovers. So this isn't that out of character."

She sighed. "I guess you're right."

"My mom almost found out that we went and looked at wedding dresses. I'm pretty sure when I actually go and try them on, she's going to have a breakdown. I know I'm her only daughter, but it's too much sometimes."

Sure, my mom had gotten to go with all of her daughters-in-law when they'd gone to pick out their dresses, but it was different for me. Ever since I was a kid, she'd been talking about my wedding and getting married. I mean, she was half the reason I was with Gus in the first place. She'd become friends with his mom and had forced us into playdates. The first few had been weird, but then we'd bonded over love of a TV show and, like kids, we'd formed a friendship based on that one thing.

I can't even remember the first time she told me I was going to marry him. It embarrassed me for a few years until I started ignoring it. Then we started dating and she was so damn happy. My dad and Gus got along so well, and I'd often find them hanging out in the kitchen when I didn't even know Gus was over, talking about movies or building cabinets or hiking.

Like with Monty, Gus had been absorbed into my family and I didn't remember a time when he wasn't around.

"Earth to Tessa" she said, waving her hand in front of the screen. I'd drifted off.

"Yeah, I'm here."

She leaned closer and I could tell she was studying my face. "Are you sure there's not something you want to talk about? You've been off in the clouds today. More than normal."

"Thanks," I said, my voice dripping with sarcasm.

"You know what I mean. I love your clouds head."

"Okay, that sounds like an insult."

Her face got soft. "It's not. I love the way you think. Why did you call?"

"I don't know. Just wanted to see you and hear your voice. And to get me out of my own head about all this wedding shit."

"You don't have to do it for them, you know. Your wedding should be about you."

I laughed. "Yeah, that only works if your family wouldn't lose their fucking shit if you eloped. I mean, my mom has been planning this damn wedding since the day she saw Gus.

We're her OTP. Is it weird? Yes. But I'm not going to disappoint her. Let her have that day. I mean, it's the least I can do."

Monty was quiet for a little while, her lips pressed together. "You still don't have to do it for her."

"That's nice to hear, but it's okay. I'm fine with making myself a little uncomfortable for a day to make my family happy. And there's Gus's family to think about too. They also want this. It'll be fun once we get to the reception." Not that we had any plans for the reception because we didn't have any concrete plans for the wedding in the first place. We should probably get on that, but Gus hadn't brought it up and I'd been waiting for him. Maybe he'd been waiting for me, since I was the bride. Not that either of us was into that whole "the bride must plan everything while the groom ignores it and watches football" kind of thing.

"I just want you to do it for you."

"Well, that's not how weddings usually are. Were you going to do your wedding for you?" I wasn't the only one who'd been engaged here.

"I mean…no. In the end, it wasn't for me. Looking back, I'm not even sure who it was for. My parents, I guess. Hoping that if I married TJ, they would finally treat me like their daughter and not the child they got stuck with."

Every time Monty talked about her parents, I had to breathe deeply so I didn't go into a rage. They'd been given the most incredible gift of a daughter, and for some reason she wasn't what they wanted, so they'd spent the entirely of her life trying to cajole her into being someone else. Monty had twisted and turned herself into a fucking pretzel, and none of it made them happy.

I was glad that she didn't see much of them these days and had cut off most contact. Every time she saw them, it took her a week to recover and get back to herself.

"Your parents can go fuck themselves," I said. It wasn't the first time I'd shared that kind of sentiment.

"I don't want to talk about my parents," she said quietly.

"Sorry. Do you want to just go to bed? Or do you need me to talk?" I would, if it was what she needed.

"No, I'm fine. You called me, remember?"

"Oh, right." I settled back onto my bed and looked up at the ceiling and the faded glow-in-the-dark stars that Monty had helped me stick up there what felt like a million years ago. I'd wanted to do random patterns and she'd insisted on measuring and copying the constellations, so we'd ended up with both.

"Do you want me to talk? I can read you something," she said. That was new. Usually I was the one who did most of the talking during these kinds of calls.

"Yeah, go ahead and read me something." She turned on a light and angled the phone on her pillow so I could still see her as she read.

Monty picked a book that I'd actually been wanting to read for a while, so that worked out perfectly. It was like having my own audiobook narrator.

"I'll do one chapter a night until we finish," she said before she started.

"That sounds perfect."

I fell asleep before she got to the end of the chapter.

"WE SHOULD PROBABLY START PLANNING our wedding, don't you think?" I asked Gus, when he picked me up from the bookstore the next day. My car was getting worked on, so he'd driven me to work today and would drive me to the auto shop tomorrow to pick it up.

"Yeah, probably." See? He wasn't into it either.

"I'm serious. If we don't set a date, I'm afraid my mom is going to set it up and then surprise us with a wedding. Don't think that she wouldn't, you know what she's like."

That made him laugh. "You're right. Okay. When do you want to get married?"

I had actually thought about this and the possibilities were endless, but summer seemed the easiest, in terms of planning and getting everyone there. Plus, summer weddings were popular.

"How about next June? Like, the middle of the month. We can pick an exact day when we talk to our families, but that seems right. Right?" I had no fucking idea. It wasn't like I had a bunch of experience. This was my first wedding, but I had been around for the planning of Monty's, so at least I knew a little bit more than I did when we'd gotten engaged.

"Sounds good. I'll ask my parents what they have going on and make sure there are no holidays or anything. Happy now?"

"Sure," I said. I didn't feel any different now, locking in a time. "So, if we do a summer wedding, do you like, have a theme in mind?"

He grinned and waved at a truck driving by.

"What kind of themes are available? Like, could we have a Star Wars theme? Or a pizza theme? Or a Star Wars and pizza themed wedding?"

I smacked his shoulder.

"August, that is not what I'm talking about and you know it. I'm thinking of decorations, the colors, that kind of thing. I know you're not going to give me free rein to have control of this shit myself."

He turned onto the road where his cabin was located. I hadn't been here in a while because I'd been so busy with Monty and dealing with the end of her engagement. I had to pull my focus back to Gus. He hadn't said anything, but he'd been neglected for sure.

"You're right. Okay, let's sit down and set a budget first, and then we can go from there. How does that sound?" he asked.

"Ugh, sensible. You're too sensible and it's annoying."

"One of us has to be."

An hour later, I realized that Gus had no idea how much a wedding was going to cost.

"Are you fucking serious?" he said when I showed him a sample budget and started going over average costs of food and tents and flowers. I thought his eyes were going to fall out of his head.

"Why don't we just do it in your parent's living room and call it good? Grill some hot dogs in the backyard," he said.

I gave him a look. "You know my mother is not going to let us get away with that. What about that pretty gazebo by the lake?" Near his cabin was a hotel with cabin rentals and they had a pretty little spot that might be perfect. Plus, there was plenty of parking and if we wanted to run away, there were kayaks.

"That's an idea. There's that picnic area too, if we wanted to do a reception all in the same place. I think other people have had weddings there before, so they probably have a package. I can ask." We knew the people who owned it, because this was a small town and everyone knew everyone, so there was a high probability of us getting a good deal.

"Okay, we'll try that." I slumped back in my chair. "Wedding planning is exhausting, can we be done for tonight? I just want to watch a movie."

Pain started pounding behind my eyeballs and if I didn't relax, I was going to have a hell of a headache.

"Sure," Gus said, closing his laptop. We crashed on the couch and he brought me all the snacks and drinks I could want.

"Do you want to move in before or after the wedding?" he asked.

"I mean, after. I thought that's what we agreed on?"

"I know, but I wanted you to know that if you want to be here sooner, you could."

My stomach turned a little, thinking about that dramatic change. I definitely wasn't ready for that shit. We could deal with that later.

"No, I'm good for now. I know we've been together for a long time, but I don't want to live with anyone before we're married, you know?"

"Yeah, yeah, agreed." He nodded in a jerky way and then went back to the kitchen and didn't come back for a few minutes.

"You okay?" I asked, as he sat back down with a fresh bottle of beer.

"Yeah, I'm good. You?"

"I'm good."

Chapter Thirteen

MONTY

Planning my own wedding had been strange, but planning Tessa's was even stranger. I guess she and Gus had talked and had started making tentative plans. I wasn't jealous, exactly, but it didn't make me feel good. She didn't want to talk much about it either, so there was an unspoken moratorium on wedding talk. Her mom was all about it, so when she hung out with me, she needed a break from it.

I still hadn't come out to anyone else, including my parents or my co-workers. Still not ready, but I had skimmed a few online dating sites. Just to see what was out there.

A lot of beautiful people, that's what. Now that I was allowing myself to see who I was really attracted to, it was like the floodgates had opened.

Every time I saw a beautiful person, my brain overloaded and I couldn't function. It was really making life hard. My dreams had turned overtly sexual, and I woke up touching myself on more mornings than I didn't. Masturbation was a joy now that I wasn't forcing myself to imagine TJ.

The library was bustling in the summer, and we always

had one activity or another going on. Tessa had volunteered to come and wrangle the Story Hour for the little ones a few times, and I was so grateful. Honestly, she would have made an incredible teacher. College wasn't for Tessa, and that was okay. She'd never finished, and I knew she had guilt and embarrassment about that. There was always a chance later on she might want to go back, but I didn't think so. Working at the bookstore suited her, and she was damn good at it.

Right now she was doing the different voices for *Peter and the Wolf,* and even the most antsy kid was rapt with attention, eyes glued on her as she held the book out so they could all see the pictures.

I leaned on the doorway to the Children's Room, which was painted to look like fake stone with plastic ivy crawling on it, and the room continued with the castle theme. There was even a little tower that had a tiny slide attached to it. When kids first came in, they lost their minds.

"She's so good with them," a voice said behind me, making me jump. Lindsey stood behind me, a stack of books in her hand.

"I know," I said. "I know she's volunteering, but is there any money in the budget to maybe hire her on to help with the reading programs?" Our goals were to keep kids reading all year long, so in addition to our Summer Reading program, we did other events through the year, and we could always use more hands.

"I'll see what I can do," Lindsey said, tapping her chin with the spine of one of the books. I'd have to make sure if it went through, that she didn't tell Tessa it was my idea. Then she wouldn't do it.

A patron tapped me on the shoulder to come help with looking something up online, so I had to stop watching Tessa do her thing. By the time I was done with the patron, there were more books to reshelve, so I was in the midst of that when a voice spoke in my ear.

"Excuse me, can you tell me where I might find the books about ships?"

I turned around, my eyes already rolling. "As you know, Cin, we have an entire display of books about ships. Our patrons demand them." It was true. I hadn't had a day when someone had not come in and asked me for a book about boats. It made sense, since fishing was such a huge industry around her, but still.

"Who is this 'Cin?' I'm just another library patron, eager for knowledge." Her eyes were lit up. She'd never admit how much she loved doing story time. In less than a year she was going to have two new niblings in her family and I was almost jealous of them. I would have loved to have an aunt like Tessa when I was younger. Her whole family was so wonderful, even her brothers, who seemed like they'd be misogynistic jerks, but somehow weren't.

"You are not and you're bothering me. What is it?"

Tessa leaned on the shelves and crossed her arms. Her hair was falling on her forehead today in a rakish way.

"Well, excuse me for wondering if you wanted to take your break with me and get some coffee." Coffee. Yes. I needed coffee. My energy level had gone down considerably and I needed more if I was going to get through the rest of the afternoon.

"Fine." I abandoned the book cart and then waved at Lindsey to tell her I was taking my break. She was at the desk with one of the volunteers, showing her how to check out the books.

"She's cute," Tessa said in my ear as we waited in line to order our drinks at the café.

"Huh?" I said. I'd been pondering if I wanted to change up

my regular order, or if I wanted to stick with something reliable.

Tessa leaned closer. "The girl two people in front of us. With the glasses. Do you think she's cute?" I took a subtle look, pretending to be looking at something on my phone.

"Yeah, she's cute," I said. She definitely was. But in a too-polished kind of way. Like, I'd be afraid to touch her and mess up her perfect hair or unwrinkled clothes. I was pretty sure I wanted someone a little more approachable.

"But not your type?" Tessa said. "Have you figured out what your type is?"

"I mean, I don't know. Why do you care?" Talking about this with her made my skin itch.

"Just curious. I'm trying to be your friend here." We finally reached the front of the line and I gave the perfect girl another look. Yeah, she was beautiful, but too beautiful. Too much.

We got our coffees and I ended up trying something new: a s'mores latte. Why not?

"You coming to kickboxing with me this weekend?" she asked, sipping her vanilla and peppermint iced latte.

"I don't know, maybe. I think I'm going to redecorate my house." My new tea set was out of place with the rest of my apartment, and I felt like I needed to do a refresh.

"You should come with me to kickboxing, and then we can go shopping. We could always stop at the antique store and get some more old shit." That was a good idea.

Someone bumped into me. "Oh, I'm so sorry." I looked up to see the beautiful girl looking down at me with luminous brown eyes that took up half her face.

"It's okay," I said. Or at least I think that's what I said. I might have just made some sounds. She gave me a little nod and left.

"Your face is so red right now," Tessa said, poking my arm.

"Shut up," I said, sipping my drink and nearly choking.

A WEEK later I got the word that the library was going to hire Tessa on for a few hours of work a week helping with some of our programs. I let Lindsey send the email so Tessa wouldn't know I had a hand in it. Of course, she called me that night anyway.

"I'm guessing you had something to do with this," she said. I couldn't tell if she was upset or not.

"We needed help and I put your name in. It's not like this is coming out of the blue. You've been doing Story Hour for years. You're so good at it, Cin." All of this was true.

"You didn't have to do that," she mumbled. If she were with me right now, I know her face and ears and chest would be an intense shade of red.

"Well, I'm not in charge of that shit at the library, so I didn't. But it will be nice to see you more."

"You sure about that? Now I can just come by and annoy you anytime I want." She laughed.

"You do that anyway."

"But now I can do it more often."

"Oh god, what have I done," I said, and she laughed even more.

There was a beat of silence, and my silences with anyone else would have been awkward. Never with Tessa.

"Thanks, though. Even if you didn't have *anything* to do with it."

"Nothing at all."

"I THINK I'm going to get a cat," I said to Tessa, as we both grabbed dinner at our favorite café up the street a few days later. We'd been at a meeting for the library to help plan some new activities.

"Oh my god, can I come help you pick it out?" That was the reason I'd told her. If I wasn't careful, I knew Tessa well enough that she would shove a kitten in her pocket and try and sneak it out.

She walked next to me back to our cars parked in the library lot. The town was still trembling with energy, even though it was a little bit late. Come winter, this place would be dead after 5pm. You had to enjoy Maine summers while you had them.

"You know that this cat is also going to be my cat, right? I will make it love me." Tessa had always wanted pets, but with so many rowdy brothers, her mother had said "no way" because there were "enough animals in this house already."

"You can come over and hang out with it when you want. But I can't make any guarantees about it loving you." I'd never had a pet either, but I assumed that I would pick a cat that would like me, right?

"I wish we could go right now," Tessa said, whining. I put the bags in my car and shut the door. My salad was probably starting to wilt, but I wasn't ready to go home yet. "Oh my god." Her hands gripped my shoulders like clamps. "Can I name your cat?"

I looked into wide green eyes that blazed with excitement. How could I deny her?

"Sure?" I said.

"Yes!" She jumped in the air and started doing some sort of strange dance that involved a lot of hip movement and some arm wiggling. It was completely and totally dorky, but I couldn't stop laughing.

"You are fucking ridiculous."

"Yeah, and you're going to have a cat with the best name

ever." She did a little hair flip and I leaned against the car. I really didn't want to go home by myself.

"Want to come over for dinner?"

"Can't. Gus is coming over to do wedding shit." The dancing stopped and the corners of her mouth turned down. Dancing Tessa was gone.

"Sounds fun," I said. It did not sound fun.

"Yeah, sure." She checked her phone but made no move to leave.

"You should probably go," I said, after a few seconds of silence. A streetlight flickered across the street.

"Yeah," she said, chewing on her lip. "Okay, bye." She turned and started walking to her car without saying anything else.

"Bye," I called after her, and she gave me a wave with her arm without turning around.

Chapter Fourteen

TESSA

"I think we have to pick colors. Colors that go with the theme," I said, tapping through some pages on my laptop. Gus and I were sprawled on my bedroom floor, trying to figure out how the fuck to plan a wedding. I'd already found apps and journals and spreadsheets and honestly, it made me want to throw up.

"What are the color options?" Gus asked, looking up from his phone.

"I mean, we can do anything, but probably ones that go well together."

"You do remember that I'm colorblind, right?" he said.

"I know, but this stuff isn't really for us, is it? It's for pictures and our families and shit. Hell, we could do shades of white and gray and black, if you want. That would look really classy." Formal, but whatever. It wasn't like I cared. Sure, I had favorite colors, but when I tried to picture chair covers or bridesmaid dresses or anything, I couldn't.

"Hey, that's not a bad idea. Then everyone can wear what they want and it will look more like a nice party than a wedding. So much of them seem so uptight. We don't want that," he said.

No, we didn't. In terms of theme, I was definitely leaning more toward rustic, rather than black tie.

"Cool. White, black, and gray it is." That gave us a starting point. And we were going to have the ceremony and reception at the lake. "What do you want to eat?"

"Oh, that's fine, I'm not hungry right now," he said, and I laughed.

"For the wedding, Gus. What do you want to eat for the wedding?"

He blinked as if I'd asked him if he wanted to serve toes. "Right. There's food involved. Uhhh…"

I slammed my laptop shut. "Listen, we already figured out a venue and our colors, or lack thereof. That's enough planning for one night. We still have a year. Some people throw this stuff together at the last minute." A headache had started to camp out behind my eyelids, and if I had to think about any more decisions, I was going to scream.

"Sounds good." Gus flopped onto his back. "I bet your mom isn't going to be happy about the colors, though." Really? Were we still talking about this?

"I don't care. It's my wedding. If she wants to be invited, she'll deal."

Gus grinned at me. "You know that she would murder you, right? Well, first she would show up, and then she would murder you."

"She would. I don't know why she cares so much. We've had so many other weddings, but she's being weird because she's mother of the bride. I don't get it, because she's such a feminist and isn't about gender roles or any of that crap, but this seems to be something she's clinging to." I sighed. "It's a lot of pressure. Being the only daughter."

Gus slid closer to me. "I'm sorry. That's not really fair to you."

"It is what it is."

"Have you tried talking to her about it?"

"Not really. I love her, but she wouldn't listen."

"It's worth a shot. If this isn't what you want."

I glanced at him. "What about you? You don't want a wedding either, but you're doing it for your parents."

"That's different."

I nudged him with my shoulder. "How? You're caving to parental pressure, just like me."

"It *is* different," he insisted.

"Fine," I said.

The two of us didn't speak for a few moments.

"I think I'm going to head home," he said, getting up.

"Are you mad at me?" I asked.

He held his hand out to help me get up. I took it and stood.

A smile softened his face. "No, I'm not. Sorry, I just have a lot to think about, and I think I need to do that thinking alone." Gus kissed my forehead and I walked him out as he said goodnight to my parents.

"Why didn't he stay over? Or you could have gone there?" Mom asked, as Gus drove away in his noisy truck. I always knew when he was coming by the rattle.

"No reason," I said. I wasn't getting into this stuff. "I'm going to bed."

"You two aren't fighting, are you?" Mom jumped up from the couch, as if she was going to run after Gus herself and make him come back and make up with me.

"No, Mom. We're fine. Can you just lay off?" I regretted the words the instant I said them. "Sorry, I'm just tired and I'm getting a headache. Goodnight." I hugged her and Dad and headed for the shower. A hot shower always did the trick to relax me when I had too much to think about.

Once I was in bed, I scrolled through wedding pictures, looking at the beaming faces of so many people. The happiest day of their lives.

I had told myself over and over that a wedding and a marriage with Gus was what I wanted. I was going to have what these people had. We'd be happy together, forever. Meant for each other, ever since we were kids.

This was everything I'd ever wanted. Right?

I DIDN'T END up sleeping at all, and I was pissy as fuck the next day. Somehow, I made it through work, but I got a text from Gus just as I was getting into the car that he wanted me to come over. I hadn't talked with him since last night, figuring he wanted some space. I knew him well enough after all these years to sense when he needed to be by himself. Gus withdrawing was a huge red flag, and I'd honored that.

He was on the porch when I pulled up in my car, beer in hand. He held one out to me and I sat on the swing that held two people. He tipped back and forth in the rocking chair his grandfather had made, and that he'd restored.

"Are you okay?" I asked, breaking the silence.

"I'm not sure, honestly. I've been thinking about a lot." He stared out across the lake. There were still a few boats puttering around, and more than a few people swimming, diving off the docks that jutted out where land met water.

My stomach twisted.

"Are you going to tell me about this 'a lot'?"

Gus faced me. "I don't think we should get married."

I couldn't breathe for a second, and then there was only one thing to say, "why?"

Gus glanced at the lake again. "I think…I don't know if I

want to get married. To anyone. This is one situation where 'it's not you, it's me,' is actually true."

I waited for him to go on as he took a long sip from his beer bottle. I held mine so hard that my fingers hurt.

"I love you, I need you to know that. But I can't love you the way you expect me to love you. I'm so sorry, Tessa."

A mosquito landed on my leg. I didn't bother to slap it away.

"What does that mean?"

Gus took a shaky breath. "I think I'm asexual. Or something like that. I'm still figuring it out myself, but I think that's where I am right now. And I need some room to explore that, and I don't think I can do that while planning a wedding to you. I'm so sorry, Tessa. I really, really am. The last thing I wanted to do was hurt you."

I sat back on the swing and tried to figure out what to say. People were coming out right and left these days. First Monty, and now Gus.

"So, you don't want to marry me?"

"That's the other part. I don't know if I want to marry *anyone*. Or if I want to be in a marriage-type relationship. Sure, I know I could have a partnership and not call it marriage, but I need to figure out what shape that would take before I try to have it with someone, if I decide I want to. I'm also not totally convinced I'm straight, either."

Holy shit, this was a lot.

"Jesus, Gus. Are you okay?"

He gave me a tight smile. "I'm supposed to be asking you that."

"Are you?"

"I'm not sure. But I think I might be better than I have been in a long time. I just didn't want to hurt you. Fuck, that was the last thing I wanted, you know that, right? I'm so sorry, Tess."

I got up from the swing and wrapped him in a hug and kissed the top of his head, and sat on his lap, the chair tilting back and forth.

"It's okay, Gus. I love you. I always have, always will." As soon as the words were out, I knew they were the right ones. "We've been together so long that I think I just…went with it. I never questioned it."

Gus's revelation was a match that had lit several small fires that started to burn inside me.

I should be a wreck. I should be a mess. I should be cursing his name and screaming and throwing shit.

I wasn't. The overwhelming feeling that crashed over me like a bucket of ice water was *relief*. Cool, sweet relief.

There would be no more planning. No more pressure. No more worrying about who to invite or whether to serve chicken or how I was going to pay for everything. I wasn't going to be moving. My life *wasn't* going to change.

"Gus, this may blow your mind, but I don't think I wanted to marry you either. You're still my second-best friend, and I will always love you. But I didn't want to marry you. Don't want to marry you." The revelation hit me so hard, I wondered if it was really happening.

How could I not have seen it?

I absolutely, definitely, did *not* want to marry Gus.

"What a pair we make, huh?" he said, smiling at me. God, I did love him, but I loved him the way I loved my brothers and my sisters-in-law. We'd gotten swept away by expectations and pressure from all angles.

"Yeah, well, at least we figured this shit out before the big day. Think of all the people who never do, or they do and they've been married for twenty years. I'm proud of you, you know. Proud of you for telling me. If you hadn't said anything, we probably would have gone through with it," I said.

Gus's arms tightened around me. "It might not have been bad. The two of us."

"It might not have. But if it's not what we want, then why would we do it?"

There it was. The reasons *for* getting married didn't outweigh the reasons not to. Even if only one of us wanted out, that was enough.

"I'll tell our parents. I'm the one who initiated," he said.

I moved a curl back from his forehead.

"We can do it together." Thinking about telling my parents made me want to throw up, but it would have to be done, sooner rather than later.

"Come on, let's go inside."

The mosquitos were starting to get bad, and my beer was lukewarm at this point. Gus led me inside and I looked around with fresh eyes. I wasn't going to be living here. This would still be the place where I'd come to hang out, and Gus would still be one of my best friends.

I did a twirl in the kitchen as he started pulling things out to make up a little snack plate like we always did.

"You look happy," he said, arranging a few pieces of cheese.

"I think I'm the happiest someone has ever been about a broken engagement. I should be sobbing and shoving ice cream in my face and plotting ways to poison you."

Gus pulled out a fresh tub of my favorite local ice cream, filled with little white chocolate caramel cups, vanilla ice cream, and fudge crunch. "We can at least make the ice cream part happen."

As we worked our way through the snacks, we devised a plan of how to tell everyone and when. Our parents would be first, then a public statement on social media. I was against that, but Gus raised a valid point that we were bound to get a ton of questions, and it was easier to get out ahead of that and present a united front so at least our version would be out there.

"I hate that we have to do that, but it makes sense. Plus, with one post we can inform a shit ton of people at once," he said.

Gus protested when I said I needed to give the ring back.

"I'm giving it back, Gus. It's yours. It belongs in your family. I couldn't keep that. You might want to use it for someone else someday."

"Maybe," he said. "It's a lot to think about. So many possibilities that I never allowed myself."

"I think I know what you mean."

GUS and I talked and talked and talked and decided that it was best for both of us to tackle our parents in the same night. He came with me first, and it actually went better than I thought it would. Yes, my mother cried and gnashed her teeth a little, but my dad got her calmed down and I convinced her this was really a mutual decision and we still loved each other, we just didn't want to be married. We'd agreed not to talk about Gus's reasons ahead of time. He would come out when he was ready.

After a while, my mom calmed down.

"Well, if you didn't want to get married, why didn't you just say so?"

Gus and I shared a look. Neither of us had an answer for her, because there was no one answer. There were layers upon layers of answers.

Finally, we progressed to his parents. I didn't have much contact with them, but they were good people. Just quiet. They took it without too much fuss, but things did get awkward and I left as soon as I could.

Gus and I hugged in the driveway of his parents' home.

"Thank you for figuring this out. And for telling me," I said. "I love you."

"I love you, too." He gave me a tight hug and then got in his truck, heading back to the cabin.

Then I realized I had to go back to my own parents and I really needed a break. So I showed up at Monty's door. At least I knocked this time.

"Hey, what are you doing here?"

"Gus and I broke up, can I stay here?"

She blinked at me a few times. "I'm sorry, what?" Monty stepped aside and I plowed my way to the couch. This had been a long fucking night. At least I didn't have to work tomorrow.

"You and Gus broke up?" Monty crouched next to the couch and took my hand. "What the hell happened?"

"Well, without going into too much detail, we decided that neither of us wanted to be married to each other. If we ever did. Fuck, I have so much to think about and I'm too tired to do anything." I lay back and rested my head on a pillow and closed my eyes. I'd never been so tired in my entire fucking life.

"That's…a lot to take in." Monty squeezed my hand and I opened my eyes and looked at her face.

"I should be sad, right? I should be fucking devastated. I should be crying on the bathroom floor in a heap. I shouldn't feel so much *relief*."

The relief was a light feeling, a free feeling. The guilt for feeling said relief was heavy, so I kept bouncing between the two.

Monty rested her chin on my arm. "I know what you mean. After all the crying and betrayal and shit, that was me. It's okay to realize that you don't want something anymore. It's okay to change your mind, Cin."

Was it? Was it okay? Everything I'd been told and had seen contradicted that. There were next to no divorces in my family.

Everyone just seemed to meet someone, get hitched, and lived happy ever after. I thought I was going to be the same. My plan had been foolproof.

"Look at us. Two broken engagements between us." Monty laughed softly.

"What a pair of losers." I was half-joking, half-serious. She wrapped a curl of my hair around her finger for a moment.

"You're not a loser, Tessa."

"Neither are you. And neither is Gus. TJ is, though. He's lower than a loser, if that's possible."

Monty smiled softly, and I could tell she was as tired as I was.

"Can I stay here tonight? I can't handle my mom's emotions right now. She's too much."

She stood up. "You can always stay here, you know that." She went to the kitchen and came back with two cups of tea, in the silver cups.

"Looks like you're getting use out of this," I said, raising the cup.

"It's so beautiful. I try to use it every day." I moved my feet so she could sit down on the edge of the couch, but then I put my feet in her lap.

"I'm glad I didn't get a wedding dress. That would have been a bitch to try and return. And we didn't book a venue or anything." Finally, my procrastination had paid off.

"Is Gus okay? I'm going to text him tomorrow."

The tea was bright and sharp, orange with hints of mint.

"Yeah, I think he's a lot more okay than he's been. We could all hang out tomorrow." I'd completely forgotten he and I had made plans to have a picnic by the lake and swim. He was also going to try and teach me how to fish, but I was dubious about that.

"Are you sure? I don't want it to be weird."

I finished my cup of tea. "No, I think he'd be glad to see you."

Monty seemed lost in thought for a while, and I was barely holding my eyes open. I somehow pushed to my feet and went to change my clothes and brush my teeth. When I came back, Monty was still a million miles away.

"You okay?" I asked.

"Yeah, just thinking." She got up so I could make up my little bed. I'd never been so excited to go to sleep.

"I'm sorry, I'd love to stay up and talk, but I literally can't. I don't know how I'm forming this sentence right now." All of my words came out as gibberish.

"Okay, goodnight, Cin," she said with a sigh, and patted my head. "Things will make more sense in the morning."

I was nearly out when I swear she leaned down and placed a kiss on my forehead, but I must have imagined it.

Chapter Fifteen

MONTY

I couldn't wrap my mind around what had happened between Tessa and Gus. It seemed unfathomable. For as long as I could remember, everyone had known the two of them would end up together. It had never really bothered me, because it was a given, a fact. As unchangeable as the rotation of the earth.

Now everything was different. I'd spent a significant amount of time wondering what I would have worn to the wedding, and what I was going to get them as a present. I'd encouraged her to have a registry to make it easier on everyone, but she'd made a face every time I'd suggested it.

I wouldn't have to do that now. Well, I still kind of wanted to give her a present. It seemed cruel that just because she'd made an adult decision that was in her best interest that she would no longer get a gift. That was the best reason to give someone a present, in my opinion.

Oh, Gus. My heart broke for him. Tessa had skirted around his reasons, but I couldn't stop my own speculations running wild when I couldn't sleep that night.

So much had changed in less than two months. What the hell was going on? My heart kept randomly racing and I couldn't find a comfortable position. At last, I got up and went to the kitchen just for something to do. Tessa was completely sacked out on the couch, moonlight from a break in the curtains painting her face. I leaned against the counter and watched her for a moment, then shook myself because that was a weird thing to do. Friends didn't watch friends sleep.

In the back of my fridge, I found a container of fancy chocolate pudding I'd forgotten I'd bought last week. Perfect. I put on a random YouTube video and ate the pudding, while begging my brain to slow down and realize it was bedtime.

No such luck. Several hours later, the pudding was gone and I was no closer to sleep, but I needed to at least make an attempt.

Tessa coughed and I sat up in bed. Should I check on her? Was she okay? She'd seemed okay earlier, but she might have just been putting on a brave face. She'd been so exhausted.

After debating for a few seconds, I got up and tiptoed out and peered around the door into the living room. Tessa sighed and rolled over, but she didn't seem to be awake. Just tossing in her sleep. I paused for a few moments, just waiting for her to settle down again. I couldn't help being concerned. Tessa was my best friend, and as much as she didn't want to make a big deal of it, a broken engagement and the end of her relationship was a big deal. Even if it was a mutual decision.

She'd completely been there for me when things had ended with TJ, and now it was my turn to be there for her. I'd do anything for her.

～

SOMEWHERE CLOSE TO dawn I finally succumbed to sleep, and it was my blaring alarm that cut through the fog and woke me.

"Fuck," I said. I'd forgotten, in my infinite wisdom, to turn off my regular alarm that I used to get up for work. I silenced it and rolled onto my back. That was when the smell coming from the kitchen hit me.

Then I heard the singing.

Curious what the hell was happening, I stumbled to my feet and pushed myself through the door and into the kitchen. What I found was not what I expected: Tessa, still in her pajamas, wearing one of my aprons, and singing into a spatula before flipping a pancake.

"What are you doing?" I asked, and she jumped.

"I am making us breakfast! I woke up with a ton of energy for some reason, so I thought I'd do this. Oh, wow, you look like shit."

"Thanks."

I sat down in one of the kitchen table chairs and watched as she set down a huge stack of blueberry pancakes, a plate of bacon, a bowl of scrambled eggs, and two glasses of ice-cold mango orange juice.

"Where's the coffee?" I croaked. A nap was definitely in my future after last night.

"I made you a latte," Tessa said, beaming and presenting me with a cup.

"Since when did you get fancy?" I asked.

"Since you got a milk frother and I went on the internet a few minutes ago to learn how to use it?" Honestly, that frother was one of my better purchases.

"This really nice, thank you." Tessa sat down with a satisfied smile and a streak of flour on her cheek.

"You're welcome," she said, pushing some of my hair back so it didn't fall in my food.

"Are you sure you're doing okay?" I asked. There was just a tiny bit of a manic edge in her eyes. I'd seen her like this before, and the only solution was to let her wear herself out, and be there when she inevitably crashed and needed me to lean on. I was well-versed in the ways of Tessa.

"Yeah, I am. I also texted Gus, and he's cool with you crashing our date. I mean, not a date, because we're not dating anymore. That is going to take some getting used to. But he'd love to see you and tell you what's been going on." I might have protested at not wanting to interfere, but if he wanted me to be there, then that was fine.

"Who am I supposed to get to take me out to dinner now?" she said, pouting as she cut up her pancakes. I spooned some eggs onto my plate.

"I mean, how often did you and Gus go out to dinner?" I couldn't remember the last time that was. They weren't super "go out to dinner" kind of people.

"That's not the point. We *could* have gone out to dinner." She shoved half a pancake in her mouth in one bite.

"I could take you out to dinner. Obviously, it wouldn't be a date. But if you want to go out, we can go out." I had a lot of free time now too, so it might be good to shake things up a bit and do some new activities. I had a tendency to get into a rut easily and not step out of my box.

"Bestfriendidate," she said, after she chewed and swallowed.

"I'm not calling it that," I said, and it was just like the other ridiculous name she'd made up for our Savannah trip.

"If I took you on a bestfriendidate, and paid, would you admit I was right?" It took me a second to remember what she was even talking about. How did she even remember? I didn't. All I knew was that I wasn't, because it was more fun to annoy her.

"Nope," I said, snatching the last piece of bacon before she could go for it.

"I will get you to admit it one day. Mark my words." Tessa pointed her fork at me and narrowed her eyes. I just chomped on my bacon in satisfaction.

~

"OH," I said, after Gus filled me in on everything going on with him. "Oh wow."

He grinned, and I realized this was the most relaxed I'd ever seen him. Even his shoulders were looser as he reclined on a blanket we'd laid out on the dock.

"Yeah, I'm still working on it," he said.

"I know what that's like," I said. Our eyes met and he nodded.

"I know you do."

Tessa was asleep, totally crashed out after her busy morning. She always took naps if she was in the sun for too long. She looked peaceful, all sprawled out everywhere. Limbs all over the place.

"I'm glad she's okay. That was the worst part. Thinking that I'd hurt her. I would have gone through with it if she had still wanted to. But I think on some level that I knew she didn't want it either, which is why I was able to talk to her. I don't know if I did it the right way, but I did my best."

I leaned my head on his shoulder. "You're a good guy, Gus. The best. You know I'm here for you, always. I know I don't have a brother, but having you is just as good."

He kissed my temple and pulled me closer. "I'm so glad Tessa has you. And that I have you, and we're all good."

"Guess we get to be in the Pride parade next year, in some capacity."

I turned on my side and looked at him. Gus closed his eyes and lay on his back.

"Huh, I guess so. I don't even know what the lesbian flag looks like. Is there one?" I should probably know that.

"Oh, yeah. There's lots of them."

This being a lesbian thing was going to require some research. Fortunately, I loved research.

Tessa snorted in her sleep and woke up suddenly, all blinky and confused.

"Hello, sleepyhead. How's it going?"

"Can we have food now?" she asked, her voice rough.

"Yeah, let's eat."

Gus got out the cooler we'd packed up earlier, since we all contributed. I made up some sandwiches while Tessa attacked a bag of chips and Gus opened sodas.

"I feel like we should be sadder about being broken up, Gus," Tessa said.

"We don't have to do what other people do, Tess," he said. "We can do whatever we want. I mean, I can get really emotional if you want me to." He screwed his face up like he was constipated, and I wasn't sure what was going on.

"What…what are you doing, I'm scared," Tessa said. "Stop it."

Gus relaxed his face and laughed. "I was trying to conjure emotions. Or tears. I don't know how actors do it."

"There's a method to it," I said. "You have to create a deep well of emotion that you can access whenever you want." They both stared at me. "What? I read a lot. I work in a library."

"I know, but usually I'm the one who knows all the random shit," Tessa said.

"I know a lot of things too," I protested, handing her a sandwich that she bit right into.

"I didn't say that you didn't."

I made another sandwich for Gus and then one for myself.

"Hey, are you mad at me?" Tessa said, touching my arm as I cut my sandwich in half. I'd removed the crusts on hers because she didn't like them and tossed them in the lake for the fish to snack on.

"No, I'm not mad," I said. "I'm just being cranky, I don't know why."

"I brought cake. That always helps with the crankies."

"I'm not a child, Tessa. I'll be fine. I'm just in a mood." I'd been in a mood since she told me about her engagement ending and I couldn't put my finger on why I was so bothered.

"Then cake will definitely help," Tessa said, pulling a plastic box out of the cooler.

"First of all, those are whoopie pies. That is not cake." Tessa narrowed her eyes and held the box to her chest.

"Firstly, they are made with cake batter, so I consider them cake. And second, now you're not getting one."

I set down my sandwich. "I didn't say I didn't want one."

"Well, you insulted them, so no cake for you." Tessa scooted away from me, glaring.

"Is this happening?" I said, looking at Gus, but he was busy eating his sandwich and ignoring both of our antics. "Can you just give me the damn whoopie pie, Cin? Seriously."

Tessa huffed, but handed me the box. "Only because you begged."

"I didn't beg," I said, pulling one of the whoopie pies out of the box. The frosting was still soft. Perfect. I shoved nearly half of it in my mouth.

"Fine, fine. God, you're in a mood today."

I just glowered at her.

"I think I'm going to take a dip, anyone else?" Gus said, getting up and stripping his shirt off. People used to ask me if I was ever jealous of Tessa for having him, or if I'd ever had a crush on Gus. I always said no, which was the truth, but no one believed me.

It made sense now.

"I'm not in the mood," I said, but Tessa got up and pulled off her shirt.

"I'll join you."

I looked away as she pulled down her shorts. Her suit was more of a short-sleeved rash guard with bottoms instead of a bikini, but it worked for her. Tessa needed a lot of cover because her skin was so sensitive to burning. If I didn't pester her, she'd forget to reapply her sunscreen. I'd set a timer in my phone to go off when she needed another coat.

Tessa and Gus took turns diving off the dock and splashing each other as I finished the whoopie pie and then decided I needed another one. There were four, so there was still one left over for Gus and Tessa.

Feeling warm and full of sugar, I lay out on the blanket and closed my eyes, listening to Gus and Tessa play in the water. A motorboat buzzed nearby, and the wind rustled the leaves in the trees. Summer had always been my favorite season. Full of lazy days and sunshine and cold popsicles and fireworks.

I WOKE up when I felt someone picking me up from the dock.

"Hey there," Gus said, smiling at me. His hair was still wet and curling from his dip in the water.

"You can put me down," I said, and he set my feet on the ground, but made sure to keep holding me up.

"I can't believe I fell asleep," I said, rubbing my head. "Did Tessa put on her sunscreen? What time is it?" The sun was definitely in a different place than when I'd closed my eyes.

"You worry too much. I'm an adult and I know how to put on sunscreen," Tessa said, slinging her arm around me.

"Good," I said. "I should probably go home. I'm not much fun today."

"Hey, you're under no obligation to be fun. Come back to the cabin. Gus is going to grill."

There wasn't a chance of saying no to that. Gus was an incredible cook, and I wasn't going to miss out.

"Fine, fine," I said, and we packed everything up and walked back to Gus's cabin.

"You okay? Really? I'm sorry I've been kind of sassy today," Tessa said, as Gus put the cooler on one shoulder to carry it.

"No, no. I don't know what's up. I'm just off, you know? Maybe I need to sleep more or something."

"Or it could be everything that happened this summer still lurking around. Grief isn't linear." That was a good point, too. "And, you did just come to a massive realization about yourself."

That was also true.

Gus put on a goofy apron that Tessa had gotten him for his last birthday and got to work putting chicken and veggies on the grill, while Tessa and I pretended to help.

The rest of the evening was slow and drowsy, with drinks, laugher, and too much good food. We all escaped from the porch when the mosquitos got too bad and went inside to watch a new movie that Gus was excited about. I didn't pay attention.

My phone dinged with a notification that someone had messaged my social media. Curious, I pulled up the message.

"Oh my god."

"What?" Tessa was instantly at my side, looking at my phone as I gasped.

"TJ's having a baby. She's having a baby. They posted the gender reveal today," I said in a voice that didn't seem like it belonged to me.

The phone shook in my hand and Tessa took it away from me.

"I'm not great at math, but if she's that far along…" Tessa trailed off. We both knew what that meant.

"I'm so glad I have an IUD," I said, trying not to cry.

"I'm so sorry, Monty," Gus said, wrapping me into a big hug.

"It's fine, it's fine," I said. "I mean, it's not. But I'm not going to focus on it."

"Fucking TJ," Tessa said.

"Fucking TJ," I agreed.

Chapter Sixteen

TESSA

"You know, for someone with a broken engagement, you seem to be taking it really well," Ron said, as we worked on unpacking a new shipment of books the next week.

"Should I be crying more?" I asked. "I mean, I didn't even cry. Is that a bad sign? I don't have enough experience in this arena."

Ron set his box cutter down and stretched his back with a groan. "Me neither. I've only ever been with Bill, and we only got married for the sweet tax benefits. You should feel however you feel." He pulled a bandana out of his back pocket and blotted his forehead. "Let's take a break. I'm afraid if I do much more, I'm going to throw my back out again."

"You should definitely make Bill do this. Where is he, by the way?" He'd dipped out early in the afternoon and I hadn't seen him since.

"He went to check out a few new potential suppliers so we can get some more gift items in stock. I wanted to go with him, but alas." Ron pointed at the boxes and sighed.

We decided to abandon the boxes for the day and make Bill do them tomorrow.

"Hey, do you mind if I leave a tiny bit early? I want to check on Monty." I hadn't told Ron about TJ knocking up the girl he'd been cheating with, but he knew anyway because this was a small town in Maine and everyone knew everything about everyone.

"Please give her our best. I can't imagine what she's going through. I'm glad I don't see him around much anymore. I know this is rude, but he has one of those smug faces."

I laughed. "A punchable face, totally." I grabbed some goodies from the café and walked over to the library and snuck in the back and found Monty chatting with Lindsey in her office about something.

"Knock, knock," I said, when they were done. Monty looked up and her eyes were slightly less puffy than they were yesterday, so that was a good sign.

"I brought snacks," I said, holding up the bag.

She rubbed her eyes and gave me a tired smile.

"Thanks."

"Are you almost ready to go? I thought we could take a quick walk." A local group had recently cleaned up a few of the nature trails so you had less of a chance of breaking your ankle on a stray root or running into teenagers boning in the bushes.

"Sounds great. Give me fifteen."

I waited for her and shot the shit with Lindsey about books while Monty finished up what she'd been working on.

"Okay, I'm good," she said, grabbing her bag and snatching the goodies from my hand.

I drove us both to the head of the trail and we parked near a number of other cars. More likely than not, we'd run into someone we knew, which was always a risk.

Monty had already devoured all the cookies I'd picked up,

but she handed me a chocolate croissant as she rooted around in the bag for other treasures.

"Like, I know I'm a lesbian and all, and that it shouldn't bother me, but it does," she said. This newest TJ development was hitting her harder than she wanted to admit. I was trying to give her enough space to work through it.

"At least it wasn't you. That girl is stuck with him, in some capacity, for the next eighteen years."

Monty shuddered as she bit into a cherry turnover. "That's a good point."

The two of us strolled down the path, taking in the afternoon sun filtering through the trees and the subtle sounds of animals rooting around in the underbrush.

"I think I need a new apartment," she said. "I know mine is close to work, but I feel like I need a change. Something new. And maybe something bigger."

"With a nice kitchen," I added. The one in her current place was not conducive of all the cooking and baking she did.

"There's that new place outside of town that they just finished." So many people had bitched about how an apartment building would be an "eyesore" and destroy the natural beauty of the scenery.

"Yeah, maybe I'll look into it. Or see what else is out there. Not much, I'm guessing. I wouldn't want to move too far from work."

"You're not thinking of moving away, are you?" I couldn't hide the panic in my voice. Monty moving even fifteen minutes away from me would probably destroy me. That might sound dramatic, but she was my best friend.

"No, no. Of course not." She popped the last bite of turnover into her mouth and licked the excess cherry filling off her lips. "This is home for me. I don't know if I'd be comfortable anywhere else."

I knew exactly what she meant. This small, weird little place was where I belonged, and always would be home.

Not five minutes later we ran into our old school principal, then a nurse from the doctor's office, then someone from the bank.

I could tell they were fishing for info about Monty's breakup, and every single one of them knew about TJ, but they were pretending (badly) like they didn't.

It was awkward, and I hurried Monty away as soon as I could.

"I'm sorry, this was my idea," I said. "I didn't know it would be so crowded."

"It's fine," she said, and then pouted as she realized that the bag was empty. "We should probably head back anyway."

She was right, so we went back to the car.

Monty closed her eyes and leaned back in the passenger seat. "What the hell am I doing with my life?"

"Is this going to be one of those conversations, because I'm going to need some coffee first."

She opened her eyes and glared at me.

"What? I just have to have the energy for deep shit like that."

Monty stared out the window. "I'm sorry I asked."

"Hey." I touched her arm. "Sorry, that was mean. Talk to me."

"No, it's fine."

I pulled into the nearest driveway and turned off the car and faced her.

"Talk," I said.

"This is someone's driveway. They're going to wonder what the hell we're doing."

I waved my hand. "Don't worry about that."

Finally, she closed her eyes and sighed.

"I don't know, Cin. It's all too much sometimes. Realizing

that all my plans are gone, and now I have to come up with new ones, and I don't know how to do that, or where to start or what I'm supposed to be doing. Or what I even want."

I had to think about that for a moment before I answered. "I mean, I don't know what the hell I'm doing either. Does anyone? I know that's hard for you, to not have a plan, but you'll get one again. What about getting a new apartment? That's something. And getting a cat! Those are two positive things. You literally just realized you're not heterosexual like five minutes ago. Give yourself a break."

Monty nodded. "You're right. I know you're right, but my brain is telling me something else."

"Big mood," I said. My brain was always telling me all kinds of ridiculous shit that was hard to ignore. "How about this? Go home and make a list of things you want to do. Even if it seems silly. You love lists."

That made her smile. "I do love lists."

In fact, I might get her some new paper for making said lists for her birthday next month.

"Okay, I'm good. Freakout over. We can leave this random person's driveway." I'd completely forgotten about that part and then I looked up and stared right into the eyes of the woman looking out the window and glaring at me.

"Oh my god." I started the car and backed out as quickly as I could without taking out a mailbox or crashing into any oncoming traffic. It was close.

"We're lucky she didn't wave a gun at us and yell about trespassing," Monty said, but she was laughing.

"I'll think about that next time before I park in a random driveway, thanks." My heart was still racing from making eye contact with the homeowner.

Monty did seem lighter when I dropped her off at her place. She deserved to get a new apartment, and it would be fun to help her move and decorate a new place. New vibes.

I sat in my car for a few minutes before walking into my house. I'd been doing my best to avoid my mom and all of her emotions over the fact that she wasn't going to get to plan a wedding for me and Gus. She'd been even more invested in it than I'd thought.

Dad was in the living room watching Wheel of Fortune when I walked in.

"Where's Mom?" I whispered.

"She's not here," he said at a normal volume. "She's out at book club, you know that." Right, I'd forgotten.

"That's good," I said, leaning against the wall with relief. "Is she doing okay?"

"I don't want you to worry about that. She's going to be fine. How are *you* doing?" I was tired of the question, but I knew he asked it from a good place.

I pulled a light blanket off the back of the couch and lay down.

"I'm good. Do you want me to make something for dinner?"

He muted the TV. "No, I was going to order pizza. Do you want garlic bread or wings?"

"Yes."

That made him laugh. "Okay. Both it is." He kissed me on the forehead and handed me the remote before going to make the call to Charlie's.

MOM SEEMED IN GOOD SPIRITS, and maybe a little tipsy, when she got back from her book club. I remembered asking if I could join, but she told me to find my own club because it was "her" thing, which did make sense, I guess.

One of these days, Monty and I were going to start one. We talked about it all the time but had never gotten our act together. Maybe that was another thing she could add to her list.

"Can we talk?" she asked me, after she'd regaled me and Dad with the most interesting stories from book club. They did get around to discussing the book, but it usually happened after the gossip session opener.

"Yeah, sure?" I was exhausted, but I could sense she had something she wanted to get out. Dad made himself scarce, and then it was just the two of us.

"I just wanted to apologize for making you feel bad about your engagement ending. I didn't want you to think that I was disappointed in you for not going through with it. I want you to be happy, bottom line, and if you weren't happy with Gus, then I wouldn't want that for you. I love you, Tessa. I only want what's best for you." She gave me a huge hug, and when she pulled back we were both crying.

"You did make things a little dramatic," I said, as she handed me a tissue.

"Well, I wouldn't be me if I didn't cause some drama. Where do you think you get it from?" She had a valid point. The apple didn't fall far from the tree in that respect.

"I really do love you. No matter what, Tess Tess." I made a face at the nickname. My family had a whole dictionary full of embarrassing nicknames for me that I would rather no one else knew about.

"I know, Mom. I love you too."

There was a gleam in her eye. "I might have saved you a little something." She went and got her purse, pulling out something wrapped in napkins.

"Is it what I think it is?" I asked as she handed it to me.

"Check it out."

"Score," I said, as I unwrapped a small stack of Nancy's caramel apple cider cookies. They were my absolute favorite, and I'd tried to get the recipe numerous times, but she wouldn't give it up. Monty and I had spent a memorable weekend attempting to make them with limited success. Maybe we should try it again. There couldn't be anything that secret in them.

"Thank you," I said as I nibbled at one of the cookies. I wanted it to last because it would be a whole month or so before I'd get to have another one.

"You're welcome, my favorite daughter."

"I'm your only daughter."

"That I know of," she pointed out. We both laughed.

"HOW IS YOUR LIST COMING?" I asked Monty that night when she called me. I knew she would.

"Pretty good so far."

"May I add something to it?"

"Maybe? What did you want to add?"

"Figuring out Nancy's cookies again. We haven't tried for a little while. I think we can crack it if we really try."

I heard the sigh in her voice. "You really have a thing for those cookies. It would be a lot easier to just hack into her computer and see if she has it saved, or even to break into her house."

"I mean, I'm up for hacking or burglary if you are. The cookies are *that* good."

She laughed. "I mean, I know you think that, but sure, we can give the recipe another shot. I'll add that one for you."

"Nice."

There was a pause. "I was wondering if you could help me with something."

"Of course."

"I think I might want to set up an online dating profile."

I couldn't speak for a second. "Oh?"

"Yeah, I mean, it's just to test things, to see what's out there. It's not like there are a ton of eligible people in the right age bracket who are also single for me around here."

"Uh huh."

"So I was thinking I could try it. I mean, it's not a commitment or anything. It's just to try it."

"And you need my help for what?"

"I need to take a nice picture and I want you to help me with it. And maybe make sure my profile looks good?"

My chest started to tighten and I was finding it hard to breathe. What the hell was going on with me? I put a hand on my racing heart. Where was all this anxiety coming from?

"Tessa?" she asked, because I hadn't said anything in response.

"Uh, yeah. I can do that. Sure. Of course." The phone slipped in my sweaty hand and I nearly dropped it.

"Great. Thanks. I have no flipping clue if anyone is going want me, or how to go about dating someone that isn't TJ, but I figure it's worth a shot? Even if I just make a bunch of mistakes."

"Who are you and what have you done with Ford?" I asked. Monty wasn't a fan of mistakes or spontaneity or anything unplanned. I didn't know what to make of this Monty who was diving headfirst into the unknown.

She laughed. "I don't know. Let's take this one step at a time. I might turn around and completely change my mind in a day."

The conversation drifted away from her dating life and I told her about the talk with my mom.

"Well, that's good at least. Good to know that she apologized," she said.

"Yeah, definitely. I still feel like I should be more upset. Like it's going to sneak up on me or something." Could that happen? Could grief do that?

"I think you're not sad because you didn't really lose anything. You and Gus are still friends and you're doing almost the same shit you were when you were engaged. Now without the added pressure of getting married."

"True," I said. "And honestly, I don't remember the last time we kissed. You know, really kissed. Like, make out kind of thing. I figured we just weren't that kind of couple, but it turns out we weren't any kind of couple. At least not a couple that wanted to be with each other."

I couldn't even imagine trying to date again. It put knots in my stomach just thinking about it. Dating Gus was so easy because we already knew each other. There was no awkward phase. No learning about each other's families and likes and dislikes, because I already knew all that shit about him. Thinking about doing that with another guy made me want to take a nap.

"You could always try online dating with me," Monty said with a little laugh.

"Oh, hell no. I don't think so. That is definitely not for me." I shuddered at the idea of random guys messaging me and trying out their best lines. Why would I put myself through that?

"My mom probably already has a list of my potential victims and is engineering meet cutes as we speak," I said with a shudder. That's exactly something she would do.

"Oh my god, she would definitely do that. I mean, there are plenty of eligible men around. How about Rusty Collins?"

I made a gagging noise. "Are we talking about the guy who used to eat glue?"

"I'm sure he's not still eating glue, Tessa," she said.

"Hey, how do you know? Have you seen him lately? He looks like ninety miles of bad road."

Seriously, for a guy who was our age, he looked like he was

in his forties somehow. And that wouldn't have mattered, except his personality also sucked.

"You never know who could be your prince charming." I gagged again.

"Okay, okay, I get it. You don't have to do anything you don't want to, Cin. But don't close yourself off from possibilities."

"I'm definitely going to close myself off from possibilities that involve me dating Rusty Collins."

"Fair enough."

"YOU SEEM LIGHTER," Hollie said, the next time I was at their house for dinner.

"Do I?" I asked, as I cut into my second piece of lasagna.

"You do," she said, smiling at me and then beaming at Vanessa. They shared one of those secret smiles that only people who know and care deeply for one another can share.

"And we have some news. We are having a baby."

I dropped my fork.

"Oh my god, really?"

"Yes, we signed the paperwork and we have our surrogate. It's a woman we found through an agency and we're flying out to Colorado to meet her officially and go with her to the doctor."

I jumped up from the table and gathered them both in a huge hug. We all cried together.

"I'm so happy for both of you. I can't believe I'm going to have a cousin!"

"It's not for sure yet. She still has to actually get pregnant and carry to term, but she's committed to helping us do this. She's a wonderful person," Hollie said.

The rest of the meal was taken up with talk about the

potential baby, and they showed me the room that they were going to convert into a nursery if the time came.

"We're trying not to get our hopes up, but we know one way or another, we will have a child," Vanessa said, kissing Hollie on the temple.

"You're going to be great moms. I mean, you already are. You've got to practice on me and my brothers our whole lives."

"We're going to do our best. That's all anyone can do, right?" Hollie said.

"Agreed."

I STAYED MUCH LONGER with Vanessa and Hollie than I planned, but it was just so comforting and warm to be with them at their house. I couldn't stop drinking tea and eating the cookies they kept handing me.

"Something on your mind, sweetheart?" Hollie asked, after my third cup of tea.

"Not really. I mean, no more than usual, and with everything happening with Gus and now this Monty stuff."

"What Monty stuff?" Vanessa asked, as I stirred honey into my cup.

"She's like, talking about dating and it's weird. I don't know. Maybe I'm being selfish, but I don't want her to get in a relationship again. I mean, I hated TJ because he was an awful person, but I also hated him because he took her away from me. How messed up is that? I don't *own* her."

As soon as I started talking, it was as if I'd blown up a dam and the words came pouring out.

"Jealousy is normal, you know. Even between best friends," Hollie said gently, coming over to put her arm around me. "It's okay to feel what you feel."

"I don't want to feel the way I feel," I said, wrapping my

arms around my stomach. I hated the way I felt right now. It was slithery and shameful.

"Does talking about it help?" Vanessa asked.

I leaned into her. "Not really. Ask me later." Right now I wasn't feeling too great.

"It will work out eventually. Who knows what will happen?" Vanessa said.

"I'm glad TJ doesn't have a sister," I said.

Chapter Seventeen

Monty

"Okay, those are all terrible. Are you trying to make me look bad?" I said, checking the first few shots that Tessa had taken with my phone.

"Are you kidding? You look amazing. How many more do I have to take?"

I glared at her. For someone who had volunteered to be my photographer, she was really being a pain in the ass.

"Fine, whatever. Let's just go." The brick façade of the library was the perfect place, in my mind, to take a selfie that would communicate my personality to potential suitors. I'd brought several outfits and made Tessa stand watch while I changed in the back of my car and fixed my hair and makeup, and she grumbled the entire time.

"No, no. Come on. Give it to me, give it to me," she said, pretending to be an aggressive photographer. "Yes, work it, work it."

I did my best, but I knew the pictures were going to look like shit. For some reason, anytime my brain was aware a camera was on it, it sent a signal to my face to make expressions that no human had made before. As a result, all my best pictures were candids, which I couldn't very well plan.

Extremely frustrating.

"No, no. I'm done. I don't want to do this anymore." I picked at a thread in my skirt.

"Okay," Tessa said, without much protesting. "Do you want to go get something to eat? Maybe grilled cheeses from The Lobster Shack?"

"Yeah, sure." We got in my car and drove down toward the beach and parked near the food truck. In addition to amazing seafood, they also happened to make the best grilled cheese sandwiches I'd ever had in my entire life. No idea what they put in them, or what made them so magic, but they were.

"I'll buy, how's that?" Tessa said, nudging me with her shoulder.

"I'm a fan of that idea," I said as we got in line. Tessa also ordered a massive container of fries and two sodas.

Even though the picnic area was packed, we were able to find a table to ourselves that wasn't too covered in ketchup and seagull crap. I pulled a wipe out of my purse and made sure my eating and sitting areas were clear.

"Do you have one of those for me?" Tessa asked, and I gave her one. "What would I do without you?"

"Eat on a bird-shit covered bench?"

She made a face. "No, I'd probably just use a napkin or something."

I was still annoyed about the picture-taking, but it was hard to be angry with her for long.

As soon as I sunk my teeth into the sandwich, I wasn't thinking about being mad at Tessa. I wasn't thinking about my cheating ex and his new girl and baby.

"You look like you're having a religious experience over there," Tessa said, and I realized I'd closed my eyes to fully experience the wonder of cheese and toasted bread and butter and whatever else they used to make this wonderful thing.

"I can't hear you because I'm in Valhalla right now."

"Oh, is it nice there?"

"Shhhh," I said, going back to my sandwich. I thought I was going to cry when I finished, but Tessa pushed the box of fries at me.

"I didn't put ketchup all over them. You're welcome." Tessa was chaotic when it came to ketchup. I was okay with eating it in small doses, but she would literally pour it over *everything* and it ruined whatever it touched with soggy sweetness.

"Thanks," I said, grabbing a few. "Now I'm sad they're not grilled cheese."

"I'll be right back," she said, getting up.

"Where are you going?" I asked.

"Bathroom!"

I went back to my fries and waited, looking out across the dunes. The tide was high, so everyone on the beach was crammed together on a limited amount of sand. Seagulls wheeled overhead, probably looking for unattended bags of chips or snacks that they could snatch. Little fuckers.

Tessa was gone so long I thought that she was having some sort of issue, but then she came marching back with a huge grin on her face and a plate in her hand.

"There, now you can have another one." She set the still-steaming grilled cheese in front of me.

"Thank you," I said.

"You're welcome," she said, sitting back down. "Thanks for not eating all the fries." She gathered a handful and started dunking them in the bowl, yes, bowl, of ketchup she'd gotten for herself.

The second sandwich was just as magical as the first and, when I was done, I had to sit back and take a breath.

"You want to take a little walk?" Tessa asked.

"Okay."

I tied a knot in my skirt so it wouldn't get wet and we removed our shoes and carried them in our hands as we strolled through the damp sand, the waves lapping at our toes.

Tessa had her phone out and it was kind of annoying, but then she spun and took a picture of me before I could react.

"How's that?" she asked, showing me.

I was looking down at my feet, my hair billowing out behind me, and a soft smile on my lips. I wasn't looking directly at her, but that was okay.

"It's nice."

"Are you kidding? You look stunning! You should totally use this one." She sent me the picture.

"I'll think about it."

"I mean, who wouldn't want to date you?"

I leaned down to pick up a shell. "I'm guessing lots of people. What's that quote about being a ripe, juicy peach but there are still people out there who hate peaches."

"Dita von Teese," Tessa said. "I still think anyone who doesn't want to date you is wrong."

"Well, *you* don't want to date me, so what does that make you?"

"That's because you're my best friend. And I don't like girls."

She stopped walking for some reason, and I rubbed the shell between my fingers.

"Right," I said.

A moment of... something passed between us, and then she abruptly started walking again, really fast.

"Wait for me," I said, jogging to keep up.

∾

AFTER WALKING ON THE BEACH, I drove Tessa back to the library where her car was. A tense silence had fallen between us, and I wasn't sure how to fix it.

"I really think you should use that picture on your profile," she said. "You looked really good."

"Thanks, I'll think about it."

She looked out the windshield and made no move to get out and go to her car. Like there was something else she wanted to say, and it was on the tip of her tongue, but she couldn't get it out.

"Wait, what was that?" She turned and looked out the open window. "Do you hear that?"

I heard a very soft tiny sound. Tessa got out of the car and I followed her over to one of the bushes where the sound was coming from.

"Oh my god, look," Tessa said, crouching down and pulling something out from behind the bush. I leaned down to see what she had in her arms and gasped.

"Hello little one." Squirming in Tessa's hands was a cat with completely black fur and huge blinking green eyes.

"Oh, you're so little," Tessa said, snuggling the creature close as it cried. "I'm guessing it's a stray. No collar and I think it needs to be fed. Don't you, sweet baby?" The last part was addressed to the kitty. "You're skin and bones."

"Can I see them?" I asked, and Tessa relinquished her charge. The little body was thin, and its eyes were a little crusty.

"We should probably take it to the vet or something." I looked around, but there was no one nearby. The library was right on a main road, so I didn't think it was fair to leave the poor thing, even if it had been in good health.

The little ball of fur trembled and then emitted a tiny buzzing noise of a purr.

"Aw, they love you." I looked down into the kitty's face and they blinked up at me and meowed once.

"Do you want to come home with me tonight?" I asked it. The cat meowed loudly again, which made Tessa and I laugh.

"Let's go get you some food and water, you're so fragile. Can you call the emergency vet and ask what we should do until we can bring them in?"

She got on the phone and held the cat in her lap as I drove home. The little thing cried for a little while and then curled up in Tessa's lap. I hoped it didn't have fleas.

Tessa talked with a vet tech and relayed the info to me on how to care for the creature until we could get to the vet tomorrow.

Once we got to my place, we immediately got the kitty some food and water. Tessa kept looking on her phone and looking back at the kitten, lifting its tail a few times.

"What are you doing?" I asked as the cat wolfed down food so fast I thought it was going to choke.

"I think it's a girl. I think. I guess we'll find out. She's so thin."

She was, and it worried me.

"I wonder if she was a stray or what her story is," I said.

"Well, it says that we have to make a good-faith effort to find her owner, but I'm not returning a cat to someone who didn't feed it," Tessa said. She'd done a ton of quick research on her phone.

"We can ask the vet for advice." I wasn't going to get attached. Not yet. This wasn't how I'd planned to get a cat, so it definitely wasn't a sure thing yet.

"You're very cute," I said to the cat, once she'd finished drinking water. She meowed at me and I watched as she started to tentatively explore. I would have thought she'd be scared, but she seemed pretty adventurous.

I pulled out all the cat toys and bedding and other items I'd gotten in preparation.

"I think you overdid it a little, Ford," Tessa said, looking at the pile of toys I'd laid out on the floor for the cat to choose from.

"Have you met me before? I'm always prepared."

"Good point."

We sat on the floor and watched her explore and then climb in the bed and fall asleep with a little sigh.

"This sounds really weird, but can I stay tonight? I want to make sure she's okay. I know she's not my cat."

"She's not my cat either."

Tessa grinned. "Not yet."

THE CAT WAS about a year old, and other than being a little underfed, she didn't have fleas, or any other issues. No microchip, so it was unlikely someone was looking for her, but you never knew, so we agreed to do our best to find if she belonged to someone. She hadn't been fixed either, so if we couldn't find her owner, and I wanted to keep her, we'd have to get that done as well.

Tessa came with me to the appointment and took notes on everything. She was more into this than I was, and it was kind of cute. She and the cat had already bonded, and I would bet everything I owned that Tessa was already trying out names.

The rest of the day was spent making up a little FOUND CAT poster and putting it on the various local groups who dealt with lost animals, as well as the local cat sanctuary.

"She's just so sweet," Tessa said, as the cat napped on her chest in the sun.

"She is." I stared at the two of them and felt something warm bloom in my chest. "Don't name her yet."

"What? I haven't even been thinking about names."

"Liar."

She rolled her eyes. "Okay, fine. I have a list of potentials. But I really need to spend more time with her to figure out which one best suits her personality."

Of course she did. Tessa could never do something as simple as name a cat in a few hours. It required serious study. Names were important things.

∾

I SPENT Monday totally worried about the cat being alone at my house. Torn between worrying that something would happen to her, or that she would destroy my entire home without me around to stop her.

Relief flooded in when I got home and she ran to the door to greet me with a meow, and everything in the house seemed to be in order. I made some tea and she sat in my lap as I drank it.

"This is nice, isn't it?" I said. She stretched out her paws and then curled back in like a little black ball.

Another text message came in from Tessa, demanding cat updates. She'd even gone so far as to go to my house during her lunch break to check on the kitty, which I thought was a little bit of overkill.

I sent Tessa a picture and went back to my tea and searching for new apartments. There weren't a whole lot of choices in my area, so I'd have to be vigilant and jump on anything that opened up.

I pulled up the draft of my online dating profile that I'd been fiddling with here and there. I'd decided to use the picture Tessa had taken at the beach, so now I had to figure out how to talk about myself, which was an impossible task.

What did I say? What would be interesting? My life was quiet and mundane. Who would want to sign up for this? I'd also only ever been with TJ, so I might as well have zero dating experience, since everything with TJ had just been going through the motions. Fuck, I didn't even know how to kiss.

How am I supposed to date? I have no idea what I'm doing. I sent the message to Tessa.

You think I know what I'm doing? I know nothing. That was true. Neither of us had much experience.

I wish there was some sort of class I could attend or something. Dating practice.

She sent back a laughing emoji. **OMG, can you imagine? That would be hilarious.**

Why is this so hard? Is this easy for other people? The kitty started twitching in her sleep.

IDK, it's really annoying. Hey, why don't we go on a fake date? Practice on each other.

I thought about that idea for a minute. It wasn't a bad one. I was comfortable with Tessa, so it wouldn't be awkward, but I could get out some of my jitters.

I'm in. When?

GETTING DRESSED for a fake date was easier said than done. I wanted to treat this as real as possible, so I started with picking out an outfit.

"What do you think?" I asked the cat that was now officially mine. No one had come forward to claim her, so by default, I had a cat now.

I'd laid out five different dresses on my bed and was hoping Kitty would help me pick. That was what I'd been calling her, since Tessa was still working on her name and I'd promised she could name her.

Kitty jumped up on the bed, walked in a circle, and laid down on the dress that I'd just bought. It was simple, with a high neck and a skirt that went past my knees in a beautiful shade of emerald. I'd seen it in an online auction and it just happened to be my size, so I'd taken a risk and snapped it up.

"Good choice," I said, and then I had to shoo the cat off the dress and go at it with a lint brush. Having cat hair all over everything was something I hadn't anticipated when I'd thought about getting a pet. Oh well, it was a small price to pay for having such a sweet bundle of love in my life.

Kitty loved to follow me around and "talk" to me. I would respond back and we'd have little conversations. She slept in my bed right next to me, and every morning when I woke up, I'd find her there and waiting for me to fill her bowl. The two of us had settled into a routine and I almost couldn't remember what it was like before I had her.

"Are you going to be good when I leave and go on a practice date?" I asked her.

She stretched out her front paws and closed her eyes. I hoped that was a yes. So far, no destruction, other than a few things she'd knocked over here and there. She really was a great cat.

I put my dress on and did my makeup and hair. For some reason, I wanted to take my time and really look amazing. I hadn't dressed up like this in a while. Probably since we'd gone to Savannah. TJ had never been into going anywhere fancy and considered anything besides jeans or work pants "dressy" and refused to wear them. If I ever suggested going anywhere nice, he would just grunt and suggest a local chain, or a bar, or staying home. Or he'd cancel the date for an unspecified reason.

In hindsight, there were boxes full of red flags that I ignored because I was stubborn and I'd set my mind on having a husband. Thinking about how much time I'd wasted on him made me want to throw up, so I tried not to.

"Okay, no more maudlin thoughts," I said to my reflection

in the mirror. I did a little twirl and took a few mirror pictures to document looking so nice. Not that Tessa would be impressed, but still. It felt good to look pretty.

There was a honk and I ignored it, figuring someone was just being rude and hogging a parking space downstairs. Then there was another honk and my phone dinged with a text message.

Hello, I'm here to pick you up.

What?

I went to the living room and peered out the window and saw Tessa's car parked across the street, but she was nowhere to be found. Then there was a knock at the door.

I skipped the few steps and opened the door and nearly smashed into Tessa.

"Hello. I am here to pick up Montgomery Ford for a date?"

I stumbled backwards and nearly fell over.

"You're wearing a suit."

"Yes, I am, what do you think?"

"You're wearing a suit," I said again. I'd never seen her in a suit before. I didn't know she owned one. Where did she get it from? When did she get it?

"I figured since this was a date, I should dress up. Is it bad?"

Her face fell and I shook my head.

"No, it's not bad at all."

The jacket and pants were a dark blue that was nearly black, and she'd paired it with a crisp white shirt that was cut a little low in the front. Her curls were still all over the place, but I could see that an attempt to tame them had been made.

Her eyes were smoky with liner, and she'd put some sort of highlighter on her cheeks.

"You look incredible, Cin," I said. "Seriously, wow."

"Thanks. I got an ad on my social media and got it on a

whim. My mom had to do some stuff to the jacket and the pants to make them fit, but I think she did a good job."

I was having trouble swallowing. "She did."

"And look at you! Holy crap, Ford. Is this the one you got last week? Show me the twirl."

I did and when I came back around, her face and ears were scarlet.

"You look really pretty," she said in a soft voice.

"Thanks."

A sound at our feet made us both look down.

"And you look pretty too, my dear," Tessa said, reaching down and picking up Kitty. She was obsessed with Tessa. Every time she came over, it was like I didn't exist.

"Does she have a name yet?" I asked.

"Should we tell her your name?" Tessa said, talking to Kitty.

"Yes, please."

Tessa made a fake drumroll sound with her mouth and then announced, "her name is Persephone Pumpernickel Ford."

"I'm sorry, what?" I said.

Tessa looked up at me. "Persephone Pumpernickel Ford." She said it slowly.

"Persephone Pumpernickel Ford," I repeated.

"Yes."

"Can I ask why?" Persephone Pumpernickel Ford looked at me and yawned.

"Persephone, obviously, from Greek mythology. You know, married to Hades, rules the Underworld? It just seemed right." Okay, that made sense, knowing how Tessa's brain worked.

"And Pumpernickel?"

She shrugged one shoulder "It goes with Persephone."

I found myself laughing. "Fair enough."

"Are you ready to go? As much as I want to stay and talk about Persephone, we have reservations."

This was news to me.

"Reservations? Where are we going?" Tessa had insisted on being in the driver's seat for this little venture, so I had no idea what we were doing or where we were going.

"That's for me to know and you to find out when we get there." She set Persephone down and held her arm out to me.

"Do...Am I supposed to do this?" I asked.

"You can do whatever you want to do. This is a first date and we're figuring this out."

"But you wouldn't hold out your arm to a guy. I mean, I guess you could."

Tessa kept holding her arm out and I saw her face fall. "I figured this first one could be more for you, and the next one can be for me."

Oh. I hadn't known that was what we were doing.

"Are you sure? I don't want everything to be about me."

Tessa sighed. "Ford, when is *anything* about you? You never want to be the center of attention or feel like you're taking something away from someone else. For once, just let me do this for you."

I almost opened my mouth to argue with her, but then I clenched my jaw shut.

"Okay. I'll allow it," I said.

"Good."

I grabbed my bag and took Tessa's arm as we walked down the stairs and out to her car. I looked up and down the street, hoping no one was watching. Of course, it was early evening in the middle of summer in a tourist town, so literally everyone was wandering around, going to dinner themselves, or dipping in and out of the various shops.

Tessa opened my door for me.

"Why thank you," I said as I got in and arranged my skirt

under me. She hopped in the driver's seat and handed me her phone to pick the music.

"You mean I can pick anything? *Anything?*"

Her eyes narrowed as she turned into traffic. "Yes, anything." She said the words through gritted teeth.

"A person could really take advantage of this kind of power," I said, scrolling through the options. "But I'm going to be nice."

I selected a generic playlist and I could feel Tessa breathe a sigh of relief when the first song came on and it wasn't something she hated.

"Thank you."

"You're welcome."

We reached the edge of town and she turned left to take us toward the highway to the south.

"So, Montgomery Ford, tell me a little about yourself."

"Oh, are we doing that?" I asked.

"This is a date, so we have to practice conversation, don't we?" True. Conversation was the part of dating that scared me most, second only to the sex.

"I'm not sure what to say," I said. Why was I so incredibly awkward?

"If you could only eat one kind of potato for the rest of your life, what would you pick?" she said, completely startling me. I'd expected her to ask me about my job or something.

"What are my options?"

"Mashed, hash browns, regular fries, steak fries, curly fries, uhhh…" she trailed off.

"Seasoned fries?"

"Right, I knew I was forgetting at least one. Then there are those waffle ones. And tots! You can't forget about tots. So, which one would you pick?"

That required some serious contemplation. Tessa's car

rumbled along the road and the radio played softly as I thought.

"Regular fries."

"And why is that?"

"Because they're simple and they go with everything. Not too fancy. Just fries with some salt. That's all I need."

Tessa nodded.

"And you? What would you pick?"

She grinned. "Bold of you to assume that I could ever confine myself to one expression of potato. It's an impossible question because I need different kinds of potato for different purposes."

Of course she had a complicated answer.

"Such as?" I asked.

We got so many miles out of that ridiculous potato question that I forgot that we were even on a date. A fake date. A practice date. I was surprised Tessa hadn't come up with a silly name for it, but she'd made no mention of one.

"Shit," Tessa said. "I have to stop for gas. Hold on." She exited the highway and pulled the car into a gas station.

"Sorry about that."

"It's okay, don't worry about it."

Tessa pumped the gas and then opened the door and stuck her head in. "Do you need anything inside?"

"I mean, I assume that we're eating somewhere, so other than that, I think I'm good."

"Yes, there will be food involved." She finished with the gas and hopped back in the car.

"What kind of food?" I asked.

"You're not subtle. You'll see."

So far, we were heading in the direction of Portland, but there were also a lot of towns and small cities along the way that she could be taking us to. Or perhaps she'd picked somewhere completely off the map that I didn't even know about. She'd certainly done her work to surprise me for this date. Normally I hated surprises, but this was actually okay. I was comfortable with Tessa, so that took out a lot of the anxiety about going somewhere new, in an outing that I hadn't planned every single moment of.

"You're not starving, are you?" Tessa asked as we kept driving, now with a full tank.

"No, I'm good. Just painfully curious about where you're taking me."

"I think you're going to like it."

NEARLY AN HOUR later we were in Portland, and Tessa parked her car in a garage instead of taking her chances with street parking.

Tessa led me out of the garage and onto the street. She held out her arm again, and I hesitated for a second before I took it. I guess I should get used to looking like I was on a date with a girl, even though we were just friends and not really dating. Taking Tessa's arm made something warm buzz in my chest, like lazy, contented bees, drunk on nectar.

She used her phone to navigate, but every time I tried to see where we were walking, she moved the screen so I couldn't.

"Here we are," she said, looking up at a sign under which a long line of people were waiting on the sidewalk. The building was painted in dark wood, and pretty tiny, by the looks of it from outside.

"This is supposed to be the best place," she said, going up to the person standing at a podium in the front.

"Do you have a reservation?" the hostess asked. She was so tall that it almost hurt my neck to look at her, and her shoes made me feet ache to imagine wearing them.

I was starting to feel distinctly shabby compared to her, and to the other people in line.

The hostess motioned for us to go in. The place was dimly lit, and absolutely tiny. There were only a few tables, and a long counter on one wall, with stools for seating. No wonder there was a line outside. This place could seat twenty-five people, max.

"I honestly have no idea how I got a reservation here, but it happened. This place is supposed to be the best," Tessa said in my ear.

Another hostess, equally gorgeous and dressed like she was at home in designer clothing, led us to a table that seated two and handed us menus.

I couldn't stop looking around at the other diners, wondering what they thought of me and Tessa here together. She seemed completely oblivious, getting lost in the menu and muttering to herself about what she should order.

"This is really nice," I said as we were served glasses of water. A large window in front gave a beautiful view of the street, with people constantly walking by. It was all a little over-whelming.

"The reviews were good and I figured if we were going out, we were going *out* and we might as well make the most of it." She smiled at me, but then her face fell.

"What's wrong?"

"Nothing," I said. "I don't know. I feel like everyone is looking at us together and thinking we're on a date."

"We are on a date."

"Tessa."

"No one is thinking anything because everyone else is so worried about what they're going to order or how they look that they're not thinking about us."

She reached for my hand. I let her squeeze my fingers.

"I'm fine," I said. "I guess I need to get used to being seen in public with someone."

"That's why this is good practice." She took her hand back and I focused on my menu.

"There are a lot of grilled sandwiches on here," I said.

"Why do you think I picked it? I mean, it's probably not going to reach the heights of The Lobster Shack grilled cheese, but maybe they can be second best."

I smiled at her for being so thoughtful. I ended up deciding on a tomato and goat cheese panini, Tessa got a pulled pork sandwich, and we ordered poutine for an appetizer.

"I've only ever had terrible poutine, so this better be good," I said.

"Poutine is so simple, and yet so many people mess it up."

I kept stealing looks around at the other diners, but Tessa was right: no one was looking at us. That still didn't stop me from feeling like I had the word LESBIAN on my forehead. Good thing Tessa wasn't bothered about anyone thinking she was gay.

With great fanfare, the poutine arrived and it was the real deal. Cheese curds, perfect gravy, and fries at just the right crispiness.

"I would eat buckets of this," I said, using a fork. Tessa had started using her hands, but switched when she saw what I was doing. It didn't bother me if she ate with her hands.

"Seriously," she said. "We are going to have to do a poutine tour. Or even a grilled cheese tour."

My mouth started watering at the prospect. "So much cheese."

Our entrees were just as excellent as the appetizer, and I was thoroughly enjoying myself. I even decided to order a drink. They had a Moscow Mule, but that brought back memories from the gay bar in Savannah and my weirdo behavior, so I didn't want to bring that up. I ordered a mojito instead, and Tessa did the same.

"To our first fake date," Tessa said, raising her glass. I touched it with mine, trying not to drop it.

The drink was good and boozy, and I was warm and full of cheese and with my best friend who was wearing an incredible suit. What more could you ask for?

"I'm definitely in the mood for dessert," I said, pushing my plate away and then finishing my drink.

"Absolutely. But not here."

"Why not?"

"You'll see," she said with a knowing smirk.

"You know I hate surprises."

She gave me a look.

"Okay, fine. I will go along."

There was an intense fight for the bill when it arrived.

"You can get the next one," Tessa said, holding it far out of my reach. She knew I wouldn't make a spectacle of myself in this place, so she had me there.

After she paid, we left the restaurant and Tessa had to consult her phone again. We didn't walk far before she steered me toward another small shop with an industrial feel and a line outside.

"What the hell is a potato donut?" I asked, reading the sign.

"We're going to find out," Tessa said, getting in line.

Chapter Eighteen

Tessa

I didn't care how long we had to wait, I was eating a potato donut once in my life. At least we had plenty of time to look at the menu and decide what we wanted while we waited.

After placing our orders, we waited and then were handed a box of donuts that was so fresh, I had to juggle it between my hands so I didn't burn them.

"Come on," I said, nodding toward the door. Monty followed me outside and down the cobblestone street toward the wharf. The air was sharp with the scent of ocean and just a hint of diesel from the numerous boats floating in the harbor. The sun was still pretty high in the sky for as late in the evening as it was. All signs pointed to the possibility of a spectacular sunset.

"This is perfect," Monty said, when we found a bench and pulled out the donuts. They were still pretty warm, but I blew on mine before taking a steamy bite.

"Oh my god," I said, my mouth full.

"Oh my god," Monty said a second later.

We looked at each other with wide eyes. "How is it possible that a potato donut could taste this good?" she said.

"No idea." I finished my first with just a few bites, and went for another. I was still so full from dinner, but I was going to make room. These were just too good to waste.

The two of us sat together demolishing the donuts and listening to the sounds of Portland.

Monty sighed happily and leaned back on the bench. "This is perfect. This was the perfect date, thank you."

I watched the air play with a few strands of hair that had escaped her updo. She looked happy, and it made me so emotional, I had to look away so I wouldn't cry. Monty deserved happiness. She deserved to get everything she'd ever wanted.

I threw the bag from the donut shop away and we kept walking, going down to where you could walk out over the water on a wooden pier. There was also a restaurant that looked like a boat, which I'd considered taking her to. Maybe next time. On the top deck of the restaurant was a tent, and what looked like a wedding reception. Music filtered down to us.

Nat King Cole and Natalie Cole. Beautiful.

"Hey," I said on a whim. Monty turned around and I couldn't speak for a moment.

"What?" she said.

I held my hand out. "Want to dance with me?"

She froze for a second and then nodded her head. "Okay."

It wasn't weird to dance with your date. It was completely normal.

Monty stepped toward me and there was a moment of confusion as we tried to decide what to do with our hands. We settled on her hands on my waist, mine on her shoulders.

"I haven't danced like this since high school," I said, my heart beating too fast.

"Me neither," she said, her voice a little breathy. We swayed back and forth to the soft beat of the music. I hoped she couldn't feel how sweaty my hands were.

"Are you worried about people watching us now?" I asked, and her eyes locked with mine.

"No. I'm not worried about anything right now." Ever so slightly, she leaned toward me. I was only about two inches taller than her, so our faces were almost nearly at the same level. I was hot with my jacket on, but I didn't want to let go of her to take it off.

"Thanks for taking me on this date," Monty said, her voice barely a whisper.

"You're welcome. You deserve to be taken on amazing dates. You deserve everything."

She bit her bottom lip a little bit and I was mesmerized by her mouth. Now I was the one leaning closer. Our bodies were pressed so closely together we kept bumping feet.

The song ended and we stopped dancing, but we didn't break apart. The wind blew some hair right in front of her face, and I pushed it back with my hand before she could react.

"You're so good to me, Cin," she said, and I couldn't breathe for a moment. Time stopped and crystalized and all I could see was Montgomery Ford. My best friend. The person who knew me more than I knew myself. The one who I called, even before my parents. She was everything to me.

I closed my eyes because it was too much. Looking at her right now was too much, and I couldn't take it.

My hands slipped from her, and I took a step back, attempting to give her a smile that probably looked completely and utterly fake.

"Are you ready to go?" I asked, my voice cracking.

She stared into my eyes in confusion and then nodded, rubbing her arms as if she was cold. "Yeah. I'm ready to go."

THERE WAS a lot less talking as we went back to my car in the parking garage.

I didn't know what to say to her. My best friend for my entire life, and I couldn't come up with words to say to her. What was happening to me?

She kept shivering, even though it was warm, so I shrugged off my coat and put it around her shoulders.

Once we got in the car, I put on a playlist and she stared out the window at the darkening city. We had a long drive back, and I didn't know if I could go the whole way without talking.

After about ten minutes, I broke.

"Do you want to put on a podcast?" At least with that, someone would be talking, even if it wasn't either of us in the car.

"Sure."

"Your pick," I said, being completely reckless. Monty knew I was extremely picky about podcasts and rejected nearly half I tried to listen to.

"Okay," she said, and searched through. "This is one Lindsey told me about."

It was actually a podcast that I'd listened to and liked, but hadn't heard the latest episode from. That would take us most of the way back home, thank goodness.

I kept my eyes on the highway as the sky darkened and the sun slipped below the rim of the horizon. I was acutely aware of Monty sitting in the passenger seat beside me. She kept arranging the skirt of her dress and she still had my coat on her shoulders. When I got it back, it was going to smell like her. Oranges and sage and her natural Monty smell.

The podcast helped to pass the time, and the hosts were two funny people who made pithy comments in between speaking on the subject at hand, so the time didn't drag as much as I thought it was going to.

At last, I reached the limits of Crawley, Maine. Nearly there.

The street was dead, so there was a spot right in front of Monty's apartment for me to park. I pulled in and turned off the car and the podcast.

"Do you want to come up?" she said. I looked over at her and something passed between us that made every single cell of my body heat up.

"Yeah," I said. "Yeah, I can come up."

We got out of the car and I followed her up the stairs. She fumbled with her keys and dropped them when she tried to get the door open. Persephone attacked us the second we got in, winding herself around both our legs, unsure of who to beg for attention first.

"It's okay, it's okay," Monty said, bending down, my coat slipping from her shoulders.

"Thanks for this," she said, handing it back to me. I took it and hung it up by the door. I didn't need it right now. I was too warm still. There wasn't enough air in her apartment.

"Do you want some tea?" Monty asked, walking into the kitchen.

"Yeah," I said as I gave Persephone her required attention. Her purr was so loud that the people across the street could probably hear it.

Monty brought out the silver tea set. It had become a fixture in her home and it made me so happy to see her using it every day.

Not sure what else to do, I sat on the couch with Persephone. It was nice she was black, so her fur didn't show up all over my pants as she rolled onto her back for belly pets.

Monty came back with the tea and sat next to me on the couch. She usually took the chair, so this was disorienting.

"This is good," I said about the tea. All of a sudden we'd turned into two women who didn't know each other very well who had to suffer through an awkward teatime visit like we were in an Austen novel.

I was afraid that anything I said might make things worse, so I just…didn't say anything. And neither did she.

So we sipped our tea and the only sounds were the purring cat and our breaths.

I almost slid off the couch when she put her cup down and got up. What was going on? I waited while she went to her bedroom and came back with something. Her wireless speakers?

I watched as she fiddled with her phone and messed with the speakers.

One of her favorite songs started to play. It had been her favorite for years and years. I couldn't count how many times I'd heard it in her presence.

She stood up, turned around, and took a deep breath. "Will you dance with me?"

My hand shook as I set my teacup down on the table and pushed the grumbling cat off my lap. She wasn't just asking to dance. She was asking all kinds of questions. Questions I wasn't sure I had answers for.

But this, this dance, that I could do.

This time I put one hand on her waist, and clasped her fingers with my other. She was shaking.

"Are you okay?" I asked, as we started to move with the beat of the song. My entire body throbbed and my skin was too tight.

"I'm okay when I'm with you, Cin," she said.

"I know what you mean," I murmured, and she leaned closer. Once again, we were pressed together as we danced, only this time, there was no one to see us. No one to judge.

"You know," I said, licking my lips, "you only ever kissed TJ."

She grimaced. "Don't remind me."

"What I'm saying is, you should have the opportunity to kiss someone else. Someone who actually gives a shit about you."

She tilted her chin up. "Do you have any suggestions?"

"Me," I said. "You can kiss me."

Monty closed her eyes and took a trembling breath and stopped moving. Her eyes opened.

"Okay. Kiss me."

"I'm only doing this for practice," I said, bringing my face closer.

"Right. Practice."

The only other person I'd kissed was Gus, and even though we'd probably kissed hundreds of times, I didn't think I actually knew *how*. How did you kiss the person that meant the most to you?

"It's just practice, Cin," she said. One hand reached up and raked my hair back. "It's nothing."

"Right. It's nothing." So why was it taking me so long to kiss her? As I wondered what to do, she made the decision for both of us.

Montgomery Ford pressed her lips to mine and the entire world changed.

She fit our bodies together, our lips like two puzzle pieces locking into place. As if they'd just been waiting for us to put them together.

Her lips fluttered for a moment before she inhaled and pushed herself more firmly against me. The longer we stayed connected, the more I wanted. I parted my lips without losing contact and went for it.

Monty made a sound in her throat and then I felt her fingers on my face. Pulling me closer.

I wasn't sure how it happened, but it was as if we ignited.

She kissed me harder and I pulled at her hair and fought to breathe in between trying to kiss her harder as she kissed me back and made little wanting sounds in between gasps of air.

She yanked her head back and her lips were red, her cheeks bright, and her eyes wild.

"That was more than a practice kiss," she said. My chest heaved as if I'd just run up the stairs. I could barely stand with my knees shaking so badly.

"I don't know, it was pretty good practice." I could taste her on my lips.

"Do you think, we could maybe practice kissing without having to stand?"

I nodded "Reclined Kissing. Very advanced. We should definitely cover that."

"Come on then." She stepped away from me, but kept my hand as she led me back to her bedroom.

I'd been in here countless times. Thousands of times. This felt like the first time.

Monty closed the door behind us and faced me.

"You know, before we try Reclined Kissing, we might want to warm up with Door Kissing."

She made a face. "That sounds like you're going to make out with the door."

"Well, you come up with a better name for it." She was just about to speak when I kissed her instead, stealing her words. This time I used my height to push her into the door. Full body contact. This made her moan, and I took note. I had absolutely no idea what I was doing, but I followed my instincts.

She was the one who stuck her tongue in my mouth first, though.

Gus and I had attempted kissing with tongues, but it always felt way too awkward and we stopped pretty quick. I just chalked it up to being something I just wasn't into.

Having Monty's tongue in my mouth was something completely and entirely different. She moved with purpose, with determination. As if she'd made a list ahead of time.

I clasped her hands and, on a whim, put them over her head. She made a little startled noise and I pulled back immediately.

"Is…is that okay? I don't really know what I'm doing."

"No, it's…it's good. I like it."

I drove my hips into hers and her eyes rolled back in her head.

It was definitely time for Reclined Kissing.

I pulled her off the door and pushed her backward to the bed until she fell backwards with a little gasp of surprise.

Monty pulled herself up on her elbows and looked at me.

"What are you waiting for?"

Chapter Nineteen

MONTY

Kissing Tess wasn't anything like kissing TJ. Those two actions weren't even in the same category. As far as I was concerned, tonight was my first kiss. Everything that came before it melted away into nothingness.

I could feel that she wanted me. I wanted her too. I wanted her hips against mine, her hair in my face, her chest against mine. As if our bodies had been made to fit together as a set.

I'd never been so desperate for something in my entire life as I was waiting for her to make her next move. The anticipation might kill me.

Tessa took her time, as if she knew. As if she knew it would push my buttons. I hadn't even known I *had* buttons. Until now.

Gently, she lay down beside me on the bed and rolled on her side to face me.

"Are you ready?" she asked.

"Yes," I said.

With utmost care, she moved until she was completely on top of me, the two of us melding together.

"Are you okay? Is this too much?" she asked.

"No, it's not too much."

It wasn't *enough*.

Tessa kissed me again, and the warmth that spread from the tips of my fingers to the ends of my toes was enough to scorch.

She burned me with her tongue and her hands, one sneakily pulling the hem of my dress higher and higher.

I wound my arms around her, holding her so she wouldn't go anywhere.

She made a sound of frustration and rolled off me.

"What happened?" I asked, my heart sinking.

"I'm hot," she said, ripping at her shirt and then going for her pants. We'd both taken off our shoes, but she still had socks on. In a frenzy, she tried to take off all her clothes at once and didn't get anywhere.

"Let me help." I sat up and reached for the top button on her shirt. Since it was cut so low, the first button was actually below the little space between her breasts. I undid the first button and waited.

"Keep going," she said, so I did. I kept going until there was one strip of creamy skin, dotted with freckles, visible.

"Did you tape yourself in?" I asked.

"No," she answered.

As if she'd gained some courage, she pulled the shirt off and sat in front of me.

Tessa and I had never really been naked in front of each other. I'd seen her in a bathing suit countless times, but never completely topless, and never like this.

"You're so beautiful, Tessa," I said.

"You can touch me. If you want."

I did. I'd never wanted anything more.

As slow as I dared, I let my fingertips float along her collarbone. I had touched Tessa millions of times, but this was brand new. This was revelatory.

She watched as I traced unknown patterns across her skin, moving lower to her breasts and her nipples, which stood out in the light. Her chest was smaller than mine, and it was perfect. One finger slipped along the underside of one breast and she closed her eyes, her breathing harsh.

"I like that," she said, and it was almost a question. As if she was surprised at her own reaction.

I tested touching one of her nipples and her eyes flew open. "Can you…" she trailed off.

"What do you want, Cin?" The nickname in this context made it into something darker, sexier. More intimate.

Instead of telling me, she grabbed my hand and used my fingers to pinch her nipple, her head rolling back in pleasure.

"Is that what you want?"

"Yes," she said. "*Yes.*"

Figuring two hands were better than one, I tested the other nipple and she moaned.

"More," she said.

Going on instinct, I leaned forward and took one of her nipples into my mouth. The skin was so soft and warm. I sucked and then used my teeth to nip her slightly as I worked the other with my hand.

"Fuck," she said. "Fuck, that's good."

The position was uncomfortable, so I stopped after a few moments.

"Can you lay down?" I asked, and she complied.

I had her spread out in front of me and I'd never seen anything more stunning.

Now that I had a better angle, I could use my mouth however I wanted.

So I did. I kissed her shoulders and her collarbone and the undersides of her breasts and the spot right above her belly button. Her pants prevented me from going lower.

My exploration took me back to her breasts and I paid

them ample attention, until Tessa was writing and pulling at my hair.

"Stop," she said, and I sat up.

"Sorry," I said as a reflex. "Did I hurt you?"

"No. you didn't hurt me. But this date is about you, remember? This was supposed to be your practice. So let's practice."

I got off the bed and she stood behind me and unzipped my dress, letting it fall to the floor. I had a slip on underneath.

Tessa reached down and slid the silky fabric upward, until it came all the way off.

"Before you do anything, can I just hang the dress up?" I asked.

She laughed softly, the sound sending shivers down my back.

I hung the dress and slip on the back of a chair and faced her.

"You're so fucking sexy."

I hadn't worn anything particularly alluring, but that didn't seem to matter to Tessa. Her eyes were wide as she looked me up and down.

The two of us were on the threshold, poised on the tip of a blade. Tip just a little bit, and we'd fall over the edge.

"Can I see you?" she asked, and I knew what she meant. I unhooked my bra and pulled that off, and before I could second-guess, I pulled off my underwear as well.

I was naked. I was completely naked in front of my best friend in the entire world, and she was looking at me as if she'd never seen anything so beautiful in her life. She sat back on the bed.

"You have perfect everything, Ford."

I wasn't so sure about that, but I didn't argue. I took steps toward the bed so she could reach out and touch me. Her hand stroked up and down my waist, causing shivers to break out.

She leaned forward and kissed my belly, and the sensation jolted me.

Oh.

Oh.

Tessa stood up and made her way around me, dropping a kiss here and there, with me not knowing where each one would land. It was sweet and it was torture.

Her pants rustled while she moved, and the next time she came around to face me, I pulled at them.

"Take them off," I said.

"Bossy, bossy," she said, flicking the button of the pants and then letting them fall. I hadn't really given Tessa's underwear much thought before. She wore black boy shorts, and they looked so good on her. I almost didn't want to take them off, but I saved the mental image as she pulled them down.

There we were. Two naked best friends.

"Come here," she said, and I went to her. Tessa put her arms around me and kissed me hard. Skin slid against skin as we reveled in each other. In having nothing between us.

Each touch was a bright little burst of ecstasy.

Somehow, we moved to the bed and I lay down on my back. Tessa poised above me, looking down.

"What is it?" I asked.

"I'm scared," she said.

"Scared of what?"

"Of this. Of not knowing what the fuck I'm doing. Of *you.*"

I sat up and kissed her. "Don't be scared. I don't know anything either. Let's learn together."

Tessa

I had never been so terrified in my life. She was everything and I didn't want to mess this up. I couldn't mess this up.

She kissed me and pulled me close. As my heart pounded so hard I could feel it reverberate through my entire body, she took my hand and slid it down her body.

Our tongues twisted together as I reached a warm and sacred place. She gasped into my mouth at the first brush of fingers.

Above all else, I wanted this to be good for her. I stroked her again, coating my fingers in her dampness. The fact that she was wet sent a rush of desire and a similar response in my body.

She wanted this. She wanted *me*.

Monty was so soft and so sweet, and I couldn't get enough of touching her and drinking in her responses. I got bolder, slipping one finger inside, which was easy. She drove against me, begging for more. I adjusted the angle and used the heel of my hand to add pressure outside as well as inside. Worked her as I had worked myself so many times. Just a different angle.

Feeling her get closer and closer was intoxicating. The power of getting her off was incredible. I was giving this to her. Me.

I thrust my fingers harder and faster and knew the moment she started to come by how her body squeezed my fingers. She also made the most beautiful sounds that I'd ever heard come from her mouth.

She pulsed and moaned and I soaked up every second of her pleasure as my own. Fuck, she was so gorgeous. Especially now.

Her eyes opened and she looked at me. I held up my hand and waved my fingers at her.

"Guess I do know what I'm doing."

She tried to hit me and missed, still completely wrung out from her orgasm.

"You're too sure of yourself sometimes, Cin."

"Never," I replied, and kissed her.

She pulled back after a moment and I could feel like she wanted to ask me something.

"What is it?" I asked. I hoped she wasn't regretting what we'd done. I didn't. Not for a second.

"I want to try something."

"Okay. What do you want to try?"

She hesitated a second before she answered. "I want to taste you."

I almost slid off the bed. "That is the hottest fucking thing I've ever heard in my entire fucking life."

Monty smiled. "You just said 'fucking' twice."

"It was warranted."

Now it was my turn to lay back on the bed as Monty got to do what she wanted with me. I would happily submit myself to her. She deserved to get what she wanted. Always.

All of this was so new and still scary, but I didn't want to stop. Monty gave each one of my boobs a little bite reminder before sneaking down my body. I parted my legs and let her look at me. I'd never felt more vulnerable in my life, but this was Monty. She was my safe place.

She stroked the curls of red hair between my legs and I kicked myself for not grooming better, but I hadn't known that I would need to.

"I'm sorry, I should have shaved," I said, feeling my entire body go red.

"You don't have to apologize for anything, Cin. You're beautiful, just as you are."

Instead of giving me time to protest, she scooted down further until her glorious ass was up in the air, and I was completely distracted. Advantage: Monty.

Her lips touched my lower belly and she left little kisses as she went lower and lower and lower...

The first touch of her lips was so unexpected and so good that I had to force my hips down so I didn't break her face.

She looked up at me in alarm.

"I'm okay, please continue," I said in a strangled voice.

Monty grinned. "If you insist."

I most certainly did.

Her hair fell in her face as she kissed me again and I figured I should at least be somewhat helpful, so I gathered it up in one hand.

"Hey," she said as I tugged a tiny bit.

"Sorry."

"No, it's not a bad thing." I pulled lightly again, and she made a little moaning noise.

Interesting. Very interesting.

I let her get back to her task, but I kept her hair held tight in my fist.

Moments later, I ascended to a new plane of existence as Monty set to work with her lips and her tongue. I could tell she was a little nervous at first, but after a few tries, she grew more bold. Her tongue traced a path up and down my entrance, paying special attention to my clit, but hitting other areas as well. It was good. It was all so, so good.

I was lost. Utterly and completely to Monty and her mouth. Then she added a sneaky finger as well, stroking me inside with the perfect rhythm.

I'd never had anything like this. The heat of her mouth, the insistence behind her touch, it was all for me. I knew when I was close and pressed on the back of her head to let her know and she increased her pace and I came so hard that my entire universe shifted. There was nothing before now, nothing after. Only this moment.

Waves of pleasure rolled through me like thunder, each one more intense than the last, until the storm started to abate, to calm. With a few last pulses, I opened my eyes and looked down to find Monty wearing the most satisfied smile I'd ever seen.

She licked her lips and leaned her head on my thigh.

"You're so hot when you come. And I've decided I like oral sex now. At least giving." I still had her hair in my hand, and I used it to bring her back up so I could kiss her mouth, which was wet from me.

"How do you feel about receiving?" I asked.

"I don't know yet," she said with a mischievous grin.

"Do you want to find out?"

"Hell yes."

"FORD?" I said a while later, after we had tested whether or not Monty liked receiving oral (a resounding yes, which I was still pretty smug about). Her head rested on my chest and we'd been quiet, just letting the sweat dry and our bodies rest.

"Mmmm?" she said, lifting her head to look at me. Her hair was a complete mess, and she'd never been more stunning.

"I don't think I'm heterosexual."

She tried to stifle a laugh. "I mean, you could still be. This doesn't have to mean anything."

That was the point, though. This *did* mean something. Tonight meant everything.

"No. I'm not. I'm definitely not. It never made sense before. I never got it. I couldn't see it. Holy shit, Ford."

So many thoughts exploded in my head like it was the Fourth of July and they all overlapped, but they had one message: I was NOT heterosexual. I liked women. I liked one woman in particular.

"Are you okay?" Monty asked, looking down at me.

"I think...I think I'm a lesbian too?" The minute the words were out of my mouth, I knew they were true.

"Wait, are you serious?"

"Monty. We've literally been fucking and I've never come so hard in my life. Kissing you is a revelation. Oh my god, what the hell?" I had to sit up for a minute.

"Does it feel like you're kind of dying when you realize you're a lesbian?" I said, putting my hand on my chest. My heart rate was starting to concern me.

"Hey, it's okay. You don't need to figure out everything at once." She kissed my shoulder and I closed my eyes.

"I didn't want to marry Gus because I'm a lesbian. Monty, I'm a fucking lesbian."

In one bright moment, my entire life made complete sense. Everything. All the little oddities and weirdnesses and confusing feelings. My entire relationship with Gus. Our years of being together when I never *wanted* him. When what I felt for him was only a fraction of what I felt for Monty. I wanted her.

I looked into her eyes and I saw everything. As if I'd kicked off a movie montage in my head, I saw what we could have. Waking up next to her. Making breakfast together. Sneaking kisses during work breaks. Date night every week. Getting another kitten together.

A wedding. We could have a wedding. I could stand at the end of the aisle and watch her walk toward me in a beautiful white dress. I could wear a suit if I wanted and I'd get to hold her hands and tell everyone how I felt before we promised ourselves to each other.

Every single time I'd tried to picture my wedding with Gus, it had been impossible. I couldn't imagine it. I could see every single detail with Monty.

"Cin?" she asked. I'd been off on my mental journey and I came back to her.

"Ford, I have something to tell you."

"Is it that you're a lesbian?"

I shook my head. "Not that. I love you."

"I know, I love you too."

She didn't get it. I reached out and held her face in my hands.

"I love you, Ford. I *love you*, love you. I love you in all the ways." I kissed her so she'd really get the idea. I felt her confusion until she broke the kiss and stared at me.

"You *love me*, love me?"

"Yes, you dork. I love you. In the kind of way that I want to go to bed with you every night and wake up with you every morning. I love you the way that I won't get too annoyed when I find your hair everywhere. I love you in the way that I see a future. I see our future."

She didn't get out of bed and tell me to go fuck myself, so I saw that as a good sign.

"Ford?" I still held her face. My precious Montgomery.

"I love you. *Love you*, love you." She started to laugh, and it was the most joyous sound in the world, and I started to laugh and then I realized she was crying at the same time.

"Hey, it's okay." I wiped her tears away with my hands and she smiled at me with such radiance that I could barely look at her.

"It's *you*, Cin. It's always been you."

"I feel the exact same way!"

We stared at each other in wonderment. How had this happened? There would be time to think about that later, but for right now, I had one task: to kiss the woman I loved.

PERSEPHONE INTERRUPTED US A WHILE LATER, demanding attention and more food in her bowl. Monty put on a silky robe and went to tend to her and I lay in her bed and looked up at the ceiling. The sheets were still damp from sex, and I definitely needed a shower.

Monty stuck her head through the doorway. "Hey, are you hungry?"

As soon as she said it, I realized I was famished.

"Oh my god, yes."

That made her laugh. "Okay, I'll make something up."

"Do you need any help?"

"No, I'm good. Just relax."

She came in a few minutes later with a tray, complete with teapot and cups, and a beautiful plate of treats.

"Hey, let's change the sheets," I said, before she set the tray down.

"That makes sense." We stripped the bed and I got new linens out of the closet. Feeling a little weird still being naked, I snagged another one of Monty's robes and we made the bed up again together.

We sat in bed with the tray and she made me use a bunch of paper towels so I didn't get crumbs all over the bed.

"So," she said. "What are we supposed to do now?"

I shrugged one shoulder. "I don't know, live happily ever after?"

"Cin."

I popped a grape into my mouth. "I'm serious. We can do whatever the fuck we want, including each other." I wiggled my eyebrows at her and she rolled her eyes.

"You've gotten about three hundred percent cruder in the past few hours."

"Well, I've had sex with you now. You opened my inner box of crude."

She made a face. "That's disgusting."

"Yeah, but you love me, so you love someone who's disgusting."

She threw a cracker at me.

"Really, Tessa. What the hell do we do now?"

I would rather bask in the afterglow of a lot of amazing fucking, but I guess we had to come down to reality sometime.

"Well, we can bang some more, and then I probably have to go home at some point. If we want to do this for real, together, we're going to have to tell people. I don't think we could hide this from anyone, and I don't see a reason to. I know we just did the whole engagements ending thing, but I don't want to wait to tell anyone about us. You know they're going to be thrilled."

"Not everyone," Monty said, pulling up her knees and putting her chin on them.

"My parents will be. My aunts will be. My brothers will be. Gus will be. Lindsey and Ron and Bill will be. Those are the people who matter. And we can deal with your parents or not. You don't owe them anything."

"I know," she said, trying to wipe away a few tears. "I can't stop wanting their approval."

I moved the tray aside so it wasn't between us anymore.

"It's going to be okay. You have me by your side. I won't let anyone hurt you. Not even your parents." I kissed the top of her head and held her close.

She sniffed and I pulled back.

"Can you believe it took us this long to find each other?"

"I've always loved you, even if I didn't know it. You're the one, Ford." She smiled and I kissed her again. And again. And again.

Chapter Twenty

MONTY

There was more sex, and more talking. We'd stayed up all night, so we inevitably crashed on Sunday, still naked and wrapped around each other. Best nap of my life.

The bubble had to burst, though, and we had to figure out what our next steps were.

"How about we bring everyone together so we can do it all at once? I mean, my aunts aren't here, but we can get them on video." That was Tessa's suggestion, and although it made me want to throw up, it did make sense. Do it like a bandage: all at once.

The rest of the day was spent alternately napping, inviting everyone to dinner at Tessa's house, and more sex. I was actually considering quitting my job and devoting myself to full-time sex with Tessa. I couldn't think of a better way to spend my life.

"Okay, we really need to get our shit together," Tessa said, and we headed for the shower. It was a bit of a scramble to figure out how to shower together and get clean and not get distracted by each other, but somehow we managed.

It seemed appropriate that if we were inviting everyone to a dinner that we would actually provide said dinner. Since we were exhausted from the sex, we grabbed a couple jars of alfredo sauce, a couple rotisserie chickens, some bags of salad, and a few boxes of pasta.

"Should we get cake?" Tessa asked when we were in the bakery section of the grocery store.

"Probably. I wish I had time to make something, but I literally can't right now." I was resting on the handle of the grocery cart so I didn't fall asleep in the aisle right there.

"Cheesecake medley it is," Tessa said, putting a huge box of different flavors of cheesecake bites in the cart. We added some drinks and called it good.

"How are we going to do this? Because this also means coming out, for you," I said.

"I told you, it's okay. I'm fine with it. You know I'm a leaper and not a looker." That was Tessa. Once she was in, she was completely in without looking back.

"Okay. If you're sure."

We arrived at her parent's house and I had to take a few deep breaths before walking in the house with a few bags of groceries weighing down my arms.

"So, what is this all about?" Tessa's mom asked as I set the bags down on the floor.

"Mom, stop being weird. You'll find out when everyone else does. Now let us cook." Tessa moved around her mom and started getting out pots and pans.

"Are you sure you can't give me a little hint?" she asked, hovering around. Tessa's dad was out puttering around the yard with a leaf blower.

When we'd invited everyone to this dinner, we'd made it sound like Tessa was the one with the announcement. If we'd said that both of us had one, they would have figured it out in two seconds flat.

"Mom, seriously. Chill."

She stopped asking questions, but she didn't stop sort of surveilling us and watching our conversations really closely from the living room as she pretended to read a book on her phone. Tessa was far more annoyed by it than I was.

The volume in the house went up dramatically as soon as her brothers started to arrive with their wives. Donny and Steph (they'd gotten a babysitter for Cadence), Mike and Bekah, Ben and Annabelle. Gus was there too, and it was good to see him.

Everyone crammed around the dining table as Tessa and I brought out the food.

"No garlic bread?" Donny asked, looking at the spread as we passed around a bowl of salad.

"Really?" Tessa said. "Can you just be grateful for a free meal, eat your food, and shut your face?"

"I mean, I could do that, but I don't want to."

Light bickering between the siblings peppered the meal and I tried to eat while also trying not to have a panic attack. When we'd come up with this plan, it had seemed like a good idea, but now that everyone was here, and I looked around at all of their faces, the reality of it was terrifying.

Even though I knew they loved me. Even though I knew they loved and would accept Tessa. Even though they were effectively my family, there was still a tiny seed of doubt planted in the back of my mind.

"You okay?" Gus said, nudging me with his arm. He was on my right with Tessa on my left.

"Yeah, fine. Just tired," I said. So, so tired. I wanted to sleep for an entire day.

Everything wound down and finally, Mike spoke up.

"Okay, can we get to the reason why we're here now? Not that this hasn't been great, but Bekah and I want to have an early night." He rubbed Bekah's growing belly and she yawned. Tessa's mom held up her phone, where both her aunts waved from their hotel room in Colorado.

Tessa met my eyes and I squeezed her hand under the table. It was time.

She pushed her chair back and got to her feet.

"I have an announcement to make. *We* have an announcement to make."

I took her outstretched hand and stood up. The plan was to have her tell everyone that we were together. But Tessa had never been one for those kinds of plans.

Instead, she pulled me toward her and kissed me. Right in front of her entire family. At first I was shocked, and then I melted into it and kissed her back. I forgot that we were putting on a show. I forgot that anyone else was even in the room.

She pulled back first and I swayed a little dizzily.

What greeted me when I looked away from Tessa's face were a whole lot of open mouths. Tessa's mom was actually crying, and Mike had the biggest smile on his face.

Everything happened at once.

"I knew it! Pay up!" Mike said, jumping to his feet. "I win, you lose." He pointed at Ben and Donny, who were shaking their heads. Gus enveloped me in a hug, Tessa's mom wouldn't stop crying, and the aunts were cheering on the phone.

I looked at Tessa, but she was staring at Mike. "What do you mean, 'pay up'? Did you place fucking bets?"

"Language," Tessa's mom said, blowing her nose into a napkin.

"Of course we placed bets. The only people who knew you weren't in love with each other were the two of you. We placed a bet on when you would figure it out and I said it would be tonight, so I win!" Mike pumped his fist in the air and Tessa's face darkened.

"You are *dead*, Michael O'Connell. Dead." Tessa dove at him and there was a short chase as he bolted from the dining room and headed toward the garage, maybe to escape in his car.

Tessa's dad chose that moment to wipe his face with a napkin, get up, and come to give me a hug.

"I'm so happy for you both. You've always been our second daughter. Now it's official."

I hugged him back and tried to swallow my tears, failing completely.

Mike and Tessa came back with a box. She was yelling at him.

"I can't believe you!" She held up a dusty shirt from the dusty box. It said *I love my lesbian sisters!* in the colors of the lesbian flag, which I had only recently looked up.

"When did you make those?" I asked. They looked like they had seen better days.

"Uhhhh, years ago. I put in an order for the other ones for Pride and got a good deal. I knew I'd use them eventually." He held up the shirt with a huge grin and then started throwing them at people as Tessa steamed.

I went over to her and put my arm around her.

"Hey, don't be mad. They're being supportive. In their way."

She made a growling noise deep in her throat.

It wasn't lost on me that the word "sisters" was plural. I was part of their family. Of *this* family. My family.

Once the t-shirt fight was over, it was hugs all around, and then I sat down with Tessa's aunts for a quick chat.

"I can't wait to see you again. Thank you so much for everything you've done for us," I said as Tessa and I squished next to each other on the couch so we were both in frame.

"We love you so much, and we wish we were there! We'll give you huge hugs when we get back."

They also had their own big news, since they were going tomorrow with their surrogate for implantation of the embryos at the doctor's office. If all went well, they would hopefully have at least one baby on the way in a few months.

Everyone congregated in the living room with dessert, and now that the stress was off, it was a lot easier to relax. Tessa and I sat together, her arm around me, or on my leg.

I couldn't stop touching her. I couldn't stop looking at her. I couldn't stop smiling because she was mine.

"Hey," she said in my ear.

"Hey," I said back.

"Can I stay with you tonight?"

"You'd better," I said. "I have plans."

"Ohhh, what kind of plans? Are they sexy plans?"

I looked around in horror, hoping no one was eavesdropping on us, but everyone else seemed to be having their own conversations and not paying attention to us. Gus was chatting with my dad about something, and Mom was poking at Bekah's belly. All the brothers had their heads together about something, and the other wives were swapping recipes.

"Shhh, don't say that too loud. But yes," I said.

"Lucky me."

She kissed my cheek and I blushed.

"You're so beautiful, and I can't believe it took me this long to figure everything out," she said, putting her empty plate on the coffee table.

"I know. We could have been together this whole time."

She shook her head. "We can't regret the past. Maybe it's what we needed to get us here. Maybe we needed that time."

She was right. And who knows what might have happened if we'd figured everything out sooner. There was no way to know. All I knew was that now, here, with her, everything was right.

"I think we should have a toast," Tessa's mom said, handing out small glasses of champagne that had appeared from nowhere. The pregnant ones had orange juice in their glasses.

"To Tessa and Monty. We all love you and support you, and we're so happy for you." She choked on a sob and leaned against her husband. He put his arm around her and took up where she left off.

"To Tessa and Monty!"

Glasses were raised and clinked and we all drank.

People filtered out, giving hugs and words of support and soon it was just me, Monty, and her parents.

"Now, I know this is all new," her mom said, "but I'm wondering if a wedding might be in the distant future?" Her eyes gleamed with possibilities.

"Oh my god, Mom, it's been one day, can you calm down?"

"I'm just saying! It would be so beautiful."

Tessa grabbed my hand and started dragging me from the room. "I'm staying at Monty's tonight bye!"

Epilogue

TESSA

"No, absolutely not." I got up from the chair and pouted at Monty.

"Why not? It's so cute. Just sit in it."

We were buying furniture for our new apartment together. After basically living together for a month, it was time. We'd managed to get a lease in the new building at the edge of town, and I was over the moon to decorate our place, but we were having some disagreements. Right now it was about a chair.

"It doesn't go with anything. We already agreed on a color palate," Monty said, pointing to her notebook. During our "planning meetings" as she called them, we'd gone over paint colors, furniture styles, lamps, and so many other things my head had spun. Honestly, I didn't really give a fuck, as long as she was happy. But I really wanted this chair.

Said chair was covered in pink velvet and circular shaped, so you kind of fell back into it when you sat. There was enough room to pull my feet up to get cozy, and it looked cool and modern.

"Tessa, I love you, but we have a theme. We agreed on the

theme." Monty pinched the bridge of her nose. I was going to have to get her some coffee soon, or she was going to lose it.

"Please?" I said, getting in the chair and clasping my hands together. "It's soft and pretty and Persephone would love it."

Persephone Pumpernickel, known as Seph, Kitty, Pip, and a number of other random nicknames, was *our* cat now. I couldn't wait to be with her and Monty on our own place all the time. I was also inches away from convincing Monty that we needed to get another cat so Seph wouldn't be lonely. So close.

Monty pressed her lips together, but I knew her well enough to know that she was going to cave. I had her.

"Okay, fine. But now we have to figure out where to put it."

I wasn't listening because I was doing a little happy dance to the music in the store. We added the chair to our haul for the day and then loaded everything into Monty's car. We were storing all our shit in my parent's garage until we officially moved in next weekend.

"I wonder how Gus's date is going," I said, sending him a text.

"I'm sure we're going to find out when you pester him to death for details," Monty said, but she was smiling.

"I can't help it. I am very invested in his life."

Gus had just started seeking out potential relationships online, and had been talking to someone for a little bit, and now they were on their first date. Or outing. I wasn't sure what he was calling it. I was beyond happy for him, and I hoped it went well. He'd been giddy for the past few weeks every time he'd gotten a text from them.

"I know, but give him some space," she said.

I deleted the text to Gus without sending it. "I can't help it. I was all in his business for a long time. It's a hard habit to break."

She reached out her hand and squeezed my leg. "I know."

Our own relationship had moved fast, in some people's eyes. For them, those who didn't know us, it seemed to come out of the blue. Every now and then I'd still get someone who thought I was with Gus, and then I had a very awkward conversation in the aisle with the laundry detergent at the grocery store.

For those who knew us, Monty and I getting together was obvious. Expected. "Oh yeah, that makes sense!" We didn't hide. We were perfectly fine going out in public, holding hands, kissing, and being openly a couple. My mom was subtly rooting for a wedding in the not so distant future, but we were just trying to get moved in together and we'd deal with that later. We were both kind of put off by wedding planning, for obvious reasons. I had settled into my lesbian label, and it felt completely right in every way for me. Completely comfortable.

It was so natural, so easy being with her. I didn't have to think about it. I didn't have to wonder. There was no guessing, no stress. Being with Monty was *freedom*.

"What are you thinking about?" she asked, glancing over at me. She'd coiled her braid on the back of her head in a knot today, and pinned the entire thing up. Her dress was covered in wildflowers and I couldn't wait to unzip it when we got back to her place. The dress was pretty, but naked Monty was prettier.

"You," I said. "It's usually you."

"What kind of things about me?" she asked, a little smirk on her face.

"Usually dirty stuff." That made her laugh. Our bedroom adventures had been illuminating. Turns out we were both a little kinky, in different ways. Monty loved being spanked and having her hair pulled, and I didn't say no to a little choking or nipple clamping. A whole world of sexual possibilities had opened up and we had all the time in the world to explore all the ones we wanted to. I had a riding crop shipping to her house this weekend that I planned to have a lot of fun with.

"Your mind is always in the gutter."

"That's why you like it," I said.

She sighed. "Yeah, I do. I love your dirty mind."

"Exactly."

"I love all the parts of your mind. Even the non-dirty ones."

"I love your mind, too. But mostly your body."

"Cin!" She tried to smack me, but missed. "I shouldn't have let you get that chair."

"You love the chair."

She shook her head, little wisps of hair floating around her like a dark halo. "No, I don't love the chair, but I love you."

"I love you, Ford. Even if you hate my amazing chair. Oh, and one more thing."

"What's that?"

I smiled and crossed both my legs on the dashboard. "I *was* right."

She gave me a deep sigh. "Fine. You were right."

I crowed in victory and she burst out laughing.

READ JUST ONE NIGHT, **the first book in the Castleton Hearts series, available now!**

Like this book? Reviews are SO appreciated! They can be long or short, or even just a star rating. Thank you so much!

Want another small-town romance? Try The Girl Next Door!

Sign up for my newsletter for access to free books, sales, and up-to-date news on new releases!

Acknowledgments

To say this has been a rough year is a massive understatement. I honestly can't even believe I finished writing this book. It started as a random idea that quickly bloomed into a series of scenes that were so clear, I could almost taste them. Writing this book has been a joy, a comfort, and a refuge. If I can give even a fraction of what this book has given to me during this time, then I'm satisfied.

My editor Laura is always there for me, and always keeps me laughing during the painful editing process. I miss your face.

Thanks also go to several authors who cheered me on and gave me encouragement including Magan Vernon, Tess Sharpe, Karina Halle, Molli Moran, and so many others.

Thank you to my Patrons who are somehow still with me even though I SERIOUSLY neglect it.

Thank you so everyone who supports me on social media and makes me laugh and sends me messages about how much you love my books. This job is not easy, but seeing those messages makes it all worth it.

This year, more than ever, I know the power of a love story. Of two imperfect people somehow finding something so special and valuable in this world.

About the Author

Chelsea M. Cameron is a New York Times/USA Today Best Selling author from Maine who now lives and works in Boston. She's a red velvet cake enthusiast, obsessive tea drinker, vegetarian, former cheerleader and world's worst video gamer. When not writing, she enjoys watching infomercials, singing in the car, tweeting (this one time, she was tweeted by Neil Gaiman) and playing fetch with her cat, Sassenach. She has a degree in journalism from the University of Maine, Orono that she promptly abandoned to write about the people in her own head. More often than not, these people turn out to be just as weird as she is. Connect with her on Twitter, Facebook, Instagram, Bookbub, Goodreads, and her Website.

If you liked this book, please take a few moments to **leave a review**. Authors really appreciate this and it helps new readers find books they might enjoy. Thank you!

Other books by Chelsea M. Cameron:

The Noctalis Chronicles

Fall and Rise Series

My Favorite Mistake Series

The Surrender Saga

Rules of Love Series

UnWritten

Behind Your Back Series

OTP Series

Brooks (The Benson Brothers)

The Violet Hill Series

Unveiled Attraction

Anyone but You

Didn't Stay in Vegas

Wicked Sweet

Christmas Inn Maine

Bring Her On

The Girl Next Door

Who We Could Be

Castleton Hearts Series

Who We Could Be is a work of fiction. Names, characters, places and incidents are either the product of the author's imagination or are use fictitiously. Any resemblance to actual persons, living or dead, events, business establishments or locales is entirely coincidental.

No part of this book may be reproduced, scanned or distributed in any printed or electronic form without permission. All rights reserved.

Copyright © 2020 Chelsea M. Cameron

Editing by Laura Helseth

Cover by Chelsea M. Cameron

Printed in Great Britain
by Amazon

26963332R00136